SAINT

THE NIGHTHAWK SERIES BOOK ONE

LISA LANG BLAKENEY

WRITERGIRL PRESS

LISA LANG BLAKENEY

Love reading novels featuring hot alpha men who fall for smart women? Then join MY VIP MAILING LIST at http://LisaLangBlakeney.com/VIP and get a FREE book just for joining!

Copyright © 2016 Lisa Lang Blakeney.
Second Edition Copyright © 2020 Lisa Lang Blakeney.
All rights reserved.
Published by: Writergirl Press

FOLLOW ME
Follow me on Facebook
Join my Fan Group
Follow me on Amazon
Follow me on Bookbub
Follow me on Instagram

LICENSE NOTE

This book is a work of fiction. Any similarity to real events, people, or places is entirely coincidental. All rights reserved. This book may not be reproduced or distributed in any format without the permission of the author, except in the case of brief quotations used for review.

The author acknowledges the trademarked status of products referred to in this book and acknowledges that trademarks have been used without permission.

This book contains mature content, including graphic sex. Please do not continue reading if you are under the age of 18 or if this type of content is disturbing to you.

To My Guy

BOOK LIST

The Masterson Series

Devour this addictive series about the possessive bad boy, Roman Masterson, who falls hard and fast for the girl he's promised his family to protect.

Masterson

Masterson Unleashed

Masterson In Love

Masterson Made

Joseph Loves Juliette

The King Brothers Series

Dive into this series of interconnected standalones featuring 3 alpha hot brothers and the women they lay claim to without apology.

Claimed - Camden & Jade

Indebted - Cutter & Sloan

Broken - Stone & Tiny

Promised - All King Brothers

The Nighthawk Series

Sexy & sweet sports romances set in the professional world of football. All standalones.

Saint - Saint & Sabrina

Wolf - Cooper & Ursula

Diesel - Mason & Olivia

Jett - Jett & Adrienne

Rush - Rush & Mia

The Valencia Mafia Series

Coming Soon. Get Notified!

LISA LANG BLAKENEY

MASTERSON

Meet Alpha Roman Masterson
Free For A Limited Time!

"Our passion is incredibly intense. The connection between us borders on the possessive. Our feelings are absolutely forbidden. The question now is...what the f*ck are we going to do about it?"

DOWNLOAD NOW

INTRODUCTION

"You will laugh, swoon, and your girlie parts will sing once you meet down and dirty quarterback, Saint Stevenson, the Gunslinger!"

He's the ultimate player. I'm the ultimate professional. We don't make any sense at all, until we're in bed...

I hate sports, and he is football royalty. I like quiet and predictable, but he's sex and swagger personified. I didn't particularly care for Saint Stevenson the first moment I laid eyes on him, but his warped brain seemed to process our initial meeting as foreplay.

I have a meticulous five year plan in place for

myself and my career, but now this huge, cocky, self-absorbed quarterback who I've been assigned to at work is seriously f*cking it up.

He's the ultimate player on and off the field, and it doesn't make any sense that I'm falling hard and fast for the arrogant baller; but there doesn't seem to be anything about our love story that makes any sense at all.

GUNSLINGER DEFINED

Gunslinger |ˈgənˌsliNGər|
noun *informal*

Term for a quarterback who plays in an aggressive and decisive manner by throwing deep, risky passes. These quarterbacks usually possess the strong arm needed to throw deep effectively.

CHAPTER ONE

SABRINA

A foolish person doesn't always recognize when she's crossed paths with someone she is destined to meet...

I slide myself back into my seat at the dinner table and begin nervously playing around with my order of shrimp scampi, which was left for me while I was in the restroom. I'm fidgeting around, because I'm a little uncomfortable in such a romantic setting like this with my coworker Jason. The man who I've been pining over pathetically for years, yet there's nothing even remotely romantic going on between us.

He looks up briefly to acknowledge my return, but then mouths the word "sorry" and continues a very spirited conversation on his cell phone. One that he's been having, for I swear, the last fifteen minutes, and frankly I'm bored out of my mind.

While everything about this restaurant screams date night: the lighting is low, the tables are meticulously decorated with fine, modern details, and there are affectionate couples all around me. This has ended up being more of a working dinner (for him) rather than anything resembling a date. When am I ever going to learn to stop fantasizing that one day the two of us will fall in love and become the company's power couple? We work, and he definitely flirts, but nothing romantic happens past that. Like him asking me out on an actual date.

To pass the time I return a few emails on my phone, and soon become distracted when I notice a sudden shift in the energy of the restaurant. An energy which rises high above the low frequency buzz of casual dining in the room.

The faces of the waitstaff become more animated.

Their eyes enlarged.

Their whispers growing to the level of dense chatter.

I look around and notice what or rather who the cause is. A man has entered the restaurant, and he walks into the place with distinct purpose.

To be seen.

I try to look away and mind my own business, but like others around me, I can't help myself as I continue to track the man's movements.

I'm inexplicably drawn to him.

With confident strides he follows the hostess with complete bravado towards the bar in a pair of well-fitting jeans, a black tee, and a pair of aviator shades on. His outfit perfectly complimenting his muscular frame.

There are two other behemoths flanking both sides of him as if he's someone important. Someone in need of security. Although I'm not totally sure why he'd need them, because the man looks like he could probably knock them both out or anyone else who got in his path for that matter.

Being in the business that I am, and living in New York City, my first inclination is to assume that he's some sort of celebrity, but then I second-guess that theory. With my experience, I think I would recognize him if he was one, even though he's hiding himself behind his sunglasses.

The colossal stranger stops just short of a couple of feet from our table and speaks with the two men who are with him. All three of them start laughing, but the rumble of his laugh specifically echoes through my chest.

I quickly turn and stare back into my scampi. His proximity makes me feel uneasy. So uneasy that my heart begins rapidly beating inside of my chest, like a skittish small animal that recognizes when a predator is nearby.

I continue searching my bowl of scampi for shrimp, as if I'm digging for gold, but can still see the man's legs out of my peripheral vision. Denim clad, muscular, powerful legs.

I'm not sure how I know, but I can sense him watching me. Maybe because he's stood completely still for the last few seconds. Almost as if he's watching and waiting for me to look up at him. I know I shouldn't, but I go ahead and raise my eyes anyway. Just for a moment.

I don't know exactly what's going on behind those shades of his, but a slow almost disquieting grin spreads across his face, when he catches me looking. Then he starts walking.

He walks behind me with heavy, considerable strides and as he passes by, I swear that I can feel one of his fingers briefly skimming the back of my neck, close to my hair. The brazen nature of his act startles me, and my spine is on fire. It's as if he's branded me with just one slight touch.

My fork drops from my hand with a clank on the table in surprise as my heart continues to thump powerfully. I gingerly place my hand on my chest to calm myself. For a split second, I wonder if I'm having a panic attack until I realize how ridiculous that is. How ridiculous this whole thing is. I don't even know this man.

I look across the table at Jason wondering if he notices what's going on. Thinking that maybe I've screwed up the possibility of this whole evening by taking such obvious notice of another man. I mean the whole point of me being here is to hopefully have Jason see me as more than just the "girl at work," but as usual, he's still in the middle of a heated discussion on his phone, completely unaware of anything going on around us. So that's why I decide that it might be okay if I turn my head for a moment to catch a glimpse of the intoxicating stranger one more time, and I'm amazed at the sight of him when I do.

He's magnificent. Even from the back.

And everyone in here knows it.

Including him.

Women who are sitting with each other or are with their significant others are all gawking at him. Repositioning themselves. Poking out their chests and sucking in their stomachs. Men who evidently seem to recognize his face are giving him respectful head nods. Even the hostess seems to have an extra hitch in her step knowing that this majestic beast is watching her walk from behind.

Who the heck is this guy?

"How's your scampi?"

Yikes. I didn't even notice that Jason's call was finally over.

"Oh," I fumble over my words. "Umm, it's okay."

"Just okay? You don't like it?"

"Well they were a little skimpy on the shrimp."

"I can order you something else," he offers apologetically.

"No, I better get going. I have some work to finish at home."

"Crap, I'm sorry, Sabrina. I wasn't much company tonight was I? I've been a little distracted for the past few days with a new account, which is already a pain in my ass. That's what that call was about."

Jason is always distracted with work. It's really nothing new, but it's also why he's such a great business manager. The best one at the company in my opinion. He's always going above and beyond for his clients.

"Anyone I know?"

"Some new alternative band out of Cali."

"Oh yeah, I heard a little about them from Marisol and none of it was good."

"Exactly. They're already giving me a headache and the ink is barely dry on their paperwork. I'm thinking about passing them over to Abby."

"Would you like me to handle them?"

I volunteer to take on Jason's group, not because I really want another client on my roster, but because I'm a little concerned that the first person he thought to throw extra work to was Abby and not me.

"I have no interest in you giving me the evil eye in the office everyday," Jason smiles. "And I know that would happen if I gave you this headache."

"But you'd give them to Abby?"

Jason tilts his head thoughtfully. "Only because I know one of her clients are about to jump ship to go with the Frazier Group. That's the only reason, Sabrina. I know you would do a good job with them if they were yours."

"Oh, okay." I say a little embarrassed that I even questioned him about it. Like I'm fishing for approval.

"You know you can email me anytime with whatever questions you may have about your accounts. You don't have to wait for these random dinner meetings of ours. I know it seems like I'm hectic right now, but my door is always open to you."

"I know, Jason, or what I mean to say is thank you. I will definitely reach out to you if I need to." I fumble awkwardly over my words as Jason looks at me as if I'm some sort of adorable little puppy or cute little sister.

Not an ounce of heat in his eyes.

In two seconds, I think he was about to pat my head.

"It's a shame your food wasn't good and mine is cold. This place was so highly Zagat rated." He frowns. "We'll have to pick a different location next time."

Jason's polite words don't impact me like they normally would. Not when he's just given me the big brother/little sister look just now, not to mention that I've been set a tad bit off kilter by the hot mystery man who I'm pretty sure just touched me on purpose.

"Okay," I reply, knowing very well that I don't need a repeat performance of tonight. Not only did we not get any work done, but we aren't even remotely close to a love connection. What the hell is the point of another dinner like this one?

At some point, I'm going to have to throw up the white flag, but unfortunately I'm a creature of habit. Day after day I eat the same things, listen to the same music, talk to the same friends, watch the same television shows, and yearn for the same man. That's just the way I'm built.

Especially when I have friends like Marisol. She's my superior at work and it was she who came up with the bright idea of having Jason mentor me as a way to ramp things up a notch. Since executing her plan he and I have been on three "working" dinners. Unfortunately none of them have produced many results, romantically or professionally for that matter.

"I'm going to go talk to the manager about your dinner, pay the check, and then go get the car. You wait here okay? No need for us both to walk that far."

"Sounds good," I nod with a smile.

It's not easy finding parking in the middle of Manhattan on theatre night, or any night in the city for that matter, but Jason refuses to pay parking lot prices after seven. He's thrifty like that. So we drove around for fifteen minutes to find a parking space on a street that is at least six city blocks away from the restaurant. That's why it's going to take him a good while getting the car.

It's such a gorgeous night though, it would have been kind of romantic if we had walked together to get it, but that's me trying to *wish* this into a date when it's anything but. For the few minutes that Jason and I did speak with each other, prior to him receiving his phone call, all the two of us managed to discuss tonight was work. Nothing personal. And I'm not sure, regardless of how much I wish it were different, we ever will talk about anything more than what we do for a living. It just may be all that we have in common.

While I wait for Jason to return from his long trek, from the shadows of the private rooms in the back of the restaurant, I see the tallest man on the planet moving towards my location with great purpose.

His shades are now off.

And his mesmerizing titanium colored eyes are locked on mine.

Eyes that look somewhat familiar, but I just can't quite place where I've seen them before.

"He left?" Are the only two words he gruffly asks.

His tone suggesting that we've known each other all of our lives, or that he has the right to ask me anything he wants.

"Umm, no."

"So then where's your date?"

Coworker not date, but there's no need to expound on that touchy subject with a total stranger.

"He's getting the car."

Wait—why I am answering this guy's questions?

"Short dinner," he observes with that same pompous grin across his face I saw when he first entered the restaurant.

"I didn't like my meal."

"He's all wrong for you, you know."

"What are you talking about?" I ask incredulously.

This guy has some nerve. Jason was barely out of the door before he came barreling over here crashing my dinner. No manners. No class. The only thing he has going for him are his looks. Too bad he totally knows it.

"I *said* he's completely wrong for you. Too short. Too inattentive. Too full of himself. And he took his eyes off of you. Big mistake."

"Too full of himself, huh? Unlike you?"

"Yeah, but I've got the goods to back it up," he says with a completely straight face.

"Ha. Ha." I roll my eyes.

"Do I amuse you, Miss ..."

"White."

"First name?"

This guy is a pure player.

"There's no need for first names is there? I mean I *am* on a date with another man."

"A very bad date. One that you clearly need rescuing from. Probably why you took it upon yourself to bail yourself out of it. There's nothing wrong with your dinner. You just want to go home."

"Are you calling me a liar, Mr.–"

"Stevenson," he replies with an amused look. "And yes, I'm calling you a liar. If short dude believes that you didn't like your food versus his less than entertaining company, then let's add one more thing to my list of reasons of why he's not the man for you. Too stupid."

I can see through the restaurant's front windowpane when Jason finally pulls up in his sleek, silver, S-class Mercedes Benz. A classically beautiful car for a very sophisticated man. A man that I shouldn't keep waiting. A guy who's always been a gentleman. A man whom perhaps if I bide my time, will end up seeing me for more than just a sweet girl at work who needs mentoring.

"Well it was nice chatting with you, Mr. Stevenson, but my *boyfriend* just pulled up," I say proudly.

"He's not going to even come back inside and escort you to the car? A car he apparently is using to overcompensate for something," he chuckles.

Boy he's gorgeous when he laughs.

Walk away, Sabrina.

"Believe it or not, this isn't the turn of the century. I'm a grown woman, and I don't need a guardian to escort me five feet to a car."

"You've got me there, Miss White. You are very much a grown woman in all the places that matter." His eyes rake over my body with slow deliberation.

"Let me give you a piece of advice, *sir,* and believe me when I say that I'm using that term rather loosely. You walked in here tonight with your oversized bodyguards and your darkly tinted sunglasses at eight o'clock at night as if you're someone important, but trust me when I say, that I know what important men look like, and you aren't it. You're trying *way* too hard. Not to mention that it whiffs of desperation that you're approaching a woman who is currently involved with another man. So have a nice life, all right?"

After my fantastically delivered admonishment, I stand up forgetting that I had placed my clutch handbag on my lap, and it drops to the floor with a thud. The entire contents inside splattering across the floor and underneath the table. Totally embarrassing.

"Would it be too turn of the century of me to help you pick up the mess you've made before my *desperate ass* goes on to have a nice life?" the stranger asks in a manner that's dripping with sarcasm.

I don't particularly want to, but I nod reluctantly in acceptance of his offer, because my very tapered pencil skirt fits way too snugly for me to comfortably bend and maneuver myself underneath the table in any sort of graceful way.

"Thanks," I try saying with as much sincerity as I can muster.

As he squats down to retrieve my things (super tampon included), I can't help but take a closer look at him in a most obvious way that almost makes me redden in embarrassment.

This close up there's no denying that he's a giant wall of muscle and masculinity. Larger than any other man I've ever known. But it's his swagger, his personality, his energy—which fills the restaurant in a much larger way than even the circumference of his body. It's no wonder why all eyes are on him.

I wasn't ever the type to attract the big, beautiful, confident types like him. I tend to attract the intellectual ones who are vertically impaired and riddled with insecurities. Neither type being a reliable pick for a girl like me. I like predictable. A safe bet.

I think that may be why I've liked Jason for so long. Jason is safe. Not a giant, but definitely taller than me. Intellectual but not nerdy. Confident but not cocky. And most importantly, certifiably single. There's no ex-wife or a baby momma. Which means no mess and very little risk. All statistics that a math geek like me can buy into.

I don't even have to talk to this Stevenson guy for more than three minutes to already know that he is the complete opposite of safe. He is probably everything my parents were always afraid would come knocking on their door looking to ravage their only daughter.

First of all, look at him.

I'm looking for someone to snuggle at night, not smother me. In fact he's so huge that there's no real way he's even going to be able to fit under the table to pick up my things. Although now I see that he doesn't even have to. His arms are so long that he can maneuver them easily under the table and reach for whatever's under there without too much awkward bending. It's actually kind of impressive.

And speaking of his arms.

Holy hell.

His arms are huge. The wingspan of his hands alone makes them look like they could easily smack someone into next week. His biceps are thick and muscular. Chiseled and strong. And my favorite part of a man's upper body, especially this man's body, are his forearms. Both are roped and strong and adorned with what looks like many sessions worth of intricate tribal ink. I've always liked tattoos from afar. They're not something I'd ever have the nerve to do, but I think they are beautiful. Especially when they adorn a man who's built like a tank.

"Here you go, Miss White."

He scoops up all of my things with one of his hands, while toying with me carefully using those two titanium saucers of his. Eyes that are confusing the hell out of my poor ovaries.

I've never been good at keeping a poker face, but there's no way this man needs to know how hot I think he is. I'm sure he already knows. So I bend my head slightly down in an attempt to avoid direct eye contact, as I accept the contents of my handbag and place everything back inside. He holds onto one thing though. One of my business cards.

"Sabrina White." He reads the card aloud while casually playing with it between two fingers. "That's a beautiful name for an equally beautiful woman."

I hate that the first thing that I do is start smiling after that lame line. Not a big smile, but a smile nonetheless.

His words are cliché.

His glare is obvious.

And I'm still grinning like a simpleton when I notice Jason sitting in his car, watching the two of us with a blank look across his face.

"Umm, my date is here. I have to go."

"Until next time, Sabrina White."

I watch as he slips my business card in his back pocket.

"I doubt it," I grin, although I'm somewhat flattered that he's choosing to hold onto my information, even though he and I both know that there will be no next time. I mean he looks like he eats women for breakfast (literally) then sends them on their merry way with a pat on the ass and maybe a couple of bucks for an Uber car.

But I'm not going to lie. I purposefully walk towards the exit of the restaurant with a little sway in my step, just like the hostess did earlier, because I know that he's watching. Something tells me that he likes to watch. What the hell, right? I never do stuff like this, and I'll never see him again.

As I smooth my skirt down the sides of my hips and thighs, and carefully place one stiletto heel in front of the other, I can't help but look in the glass doors ahead of me. Just to make sure that stranger danger is still checking me out, and when I do, I catch his reflection.

His platinum pupils dancing.

Looking straight at me.

And his mouth grinning shamelessly at the view of my behind.

So I sway my hips a little harder. Then turn around and give him a small wave good-bye. One that I make sure Jason can't see. And it's at that moment that I see and feel what I've been waiting for all night, except it's from the stranger's eyes instead of Jason's.

Pure. Unadulterated. Heat.

CHAPTER TWO

SAINT
Three Years Ago
Georgetown, Washington, D.C.

"You need to kill some time, Mike. She's not ready."

"She's not here yet?!"

"Naw, man. I think she's still at the hotel with the bridesmaids or something. No one's picking up their cell phones over there, but knowing her she's probably just running around driving everybody completely nuts."

"I knew I should've sent my mom over there. I swear to fucking God if she—"

"Calm down, best man. There's no way that girl is going to mess up her wedding day to Saint."

"You mean mess up her meal ticket."

"No shit talking today, Mike. You have to reel it in. This is your brother's future wife we're talking about. Just like you want respect for yours, you need to respect his choice."

"The hell you mean? There's no question about anyone respecting my wife. She's not some sleazy lounge singer looking for a benefactor, so that she won't have to get a real job."

"You know what I mean, Mike."

"All right. I guess the easiest solution is to get everybody drunk. Then no one will know just how fucking late the blushing bride really is. Including my brother."

"Good idea. I'll get the waiters to grab us some champagne."

Ten minutes later.

"Open the Dom! Does everybody have a glass? All right, all right. Listen up everyone. I just want to say a few words in a toast before our boy here walks down the aisle. Saint, you know you're one cocky son of a bitch. You always were. Even as a snot-nosed kid, you thought the sun rose and set specifically for your ass. Never thought I'd see the day that you'd get hitched. Especially this early in your career. But I guess there's no rhyme or reason to when we find our happily ever after. Sometimes we find her when we least expect it. So let's all raise our glasses to my little brother and his forever after – Adrianna."

"To Saint and Adrianna!!"

Fifteen more minutes later.

"Excuse me, Mr. Stevenson?"

"Yeah, that's me. How can I help you?"

"I think I need to speak to your brother."

"He's a little busy getting married right now. What do you want Saint for?"

"Well, umm ... I guess it's okay if I tell you. I need to show you something."

"Who are you again?"

"A guest on the bride's side. Can I just show you something? It's important."

"You better not be showing me any videos of your kid playing ball or something. This is my brother's wedding not a recruitment–"

"It's nothing like that. Just take a look at the headline on this website."

Jilted! Saint Stevenson's Fiancée Seen With Reality
Star & Singer Benjamin Luck On Wedding Day!

"You actually believe this? This is just some bullshit gossip blog looking to get more web traffic with lies. Adrianna is at the hotel getting ready as we speak. There's no way she's in, where does it say?"

"Miami, but look, there's a photo. Scroll down."

"Fuck me. It is her."

"Yeah, I'm pretty sure it is."

"How am I going to tell Saint? This is going to kill him."

A few moments later.

"Can we get the room for a minute, fellas?"

"Why are you clearing the room? What's up?"

"Have a seat. I need to talk to you."

"Right now? I'm about to get married."

"Calm down for just a second and listen. Adrianna is gone."

"What the fuck do you mean she's gone?"

"She left, bro. She's in Miami."

"What. Are. You. Talking. About?! What did you do Mikey?"

"Nothing, Saint. I swear. I'd never ruin your wedding day no matter how I feel about your girl. She must have gotten cold feet. She ran away with some rocker reality show kid. Some douche named Benjamin Luck. I'm assuming you haven't spoken to her today."

"We saw each other last night. She wanted to wait to talk until we saw each other at the alter."

"Well it looks like she jumped on a flight to Florida this morning."

"I'm calling her ass right now!"

"Wait. Don't chase her Saint. You're better than this. And isn't it better that you know what she's really like now rather than later when you're three kids deep? I mean if you really think about it– OUCH! You asshole. You just winged my head with that chair!

"Dammit, Saint, don't go trashing the entire reception hall. Our parents and their closest friends are here. Reverend Paul is in there. Don't embarrass yourself because she wasn't woman enough to end this the right way."

CRASH!

"You told me not to call her, so this is what I'm doing instead!"

Sigh

"Are you actually going to force me to kick your ass on your wedding day to get you to stop?"

"It's not my wedding day anymore!"

"Saint if you don't put that table down, I swear to God I'm going to have to put *you* down."

"I don't fucking care–"

WHAP!

CHAPTER THREE

SABRINA

Three years ago
Georgetown, Washington, D.C.

"What can I get you?"

A female bartender who is probably in her twenties, but looks like she's pushing forty because of the bags under her eyes and her leathery skin, asks me for my drink order. Problem is that I don't really drink.

It's one of the many things I have given up to stay at my goal weight which is actually pretty high for my height, so I have to be careful; but tonight I want to feel like someone other than myself. Even if it's only temporary. Even if it's just smoke and mirrors. And I know that alcohol can help me get there.

"What do you recommend?" I ask. Her face may look hard, but so is her body. So I'm guessing that she knows a thing or two about staying fit. "I want to order a drink or two tonight, but I don't want to consume a lot of extra calories."

"Do you like red wine?"

"I don't usually drink alcohol at all, so I don't particularly *like* any one thing."

"Then may I ask what's your reason for wanting to drink tonight?"

She asks her highly unusual question (for a bartender anyway) while drying the inside of a wine glass with a soft white cloth.

"A guy. Well basically *all* men."

"Understood." She smiles briefly. "Then shots are the way to go."

"Shots?"

"Yeah, it's the mixers that are highly caloric like fruit juice or soda. If you drink straight liquor I promise that you will arrive to your destination much quicker with little to show for it around your hips."

"That sounds like exactly what I'm looking for."

"Are you on a budget?"

"Not really." I'm using my company credit card tonight.

"Then Patron shots are the way to go. It's a premium tequila."

"Eww, with the worm inside?"

"Absolutely not," she snickers. "This is an upscale, smooth tasting tequila. Great for margaritas and also for shots and no worms."

Sounds like what I'm looking for.

"Okay, give me two."

"Coming right up."

I've never done shots before, although I've seen college kids do a million of them, but I was never that girl in school. I was a scholarship kid carrying a 3.9 GPA. I never had the time or inclination to spend my nights getting drunk and possibly date raped at frat parties. I was always in the library, and parties were never my scene anyway.

The bartender never introduces herself to me by name or much less cracks a smile. She's not warm and fuzzy like the ones I've seen on television shows and in movies; but at least she's helpful. Her goal is to get me drunk or at least feeling better, and I'm thinking she understands because she has some pretty interesting war stories about men of her own.

She demonstrates how I should drink my shots

for the full experience. Shaking the bar salt on my hand, then licking the salt, drinking the shot (with haste), and then chasing it by sucking on a wedge of lemon or lime. I like that there is a ritual behind this shot taking thing, so I catch on fast. The first shot makes my eyes squint, but by the third (or is it fourth) I am feeling *way* better.

I hear a group of voices coming towards the direction of the bar and my stomach drops. This is it. It has to be new guy's voice I hear among the sea of voices. I wonder if I've ingested enough liquid courage to finally talk to him about something other than mundane topics such as how the microwave works on the third floor lounge or the weather forecast.

I never quite mastered the art of flirting and because of that character flaw, I've ended up only dating a few guys, and they were all guys who I was set up with by friends. Unfortunately that has meant that I've usually ended up with guys that I'm not attracted to at all or who are complete weirdos.

I'm hoping that this is the one time that the nice, normal nerd (that's me) gets the successful, safe guy (that's new guy) and that we live happily ever after. For once I would like to be in a sweet, normal, reciprocal relationship.

Of course none of that will ever happen if I don't learn to say anything interesting when I open up my mouth. I tried about thirty minutes ago towards the end of our company dinner and it was a complete disaster. I made a fool of myself.

This must be what it feels like to be drunk, because my ears are playing tricks on me. I couldn't have heard the new guy, because none of the people that enter the bar are actually my coworkers. They are a group of very rowdy and gigantic men who all kind of look alike. I giggle to myself, because they look like they are going to completely annihilate the place by just moving around and bumping into things. They're that big.

It's pretty obvious that they're celebrating something, and the decibel level of their spirited banter grows only louder with each passing moment. This is my cue to leave. Even if my new coworker walked in right now, this noise would make it way too distracting for me to say anything to fix my earlier blunder.

"Are you with the Carson group?" The bartender asks me.

"Yes, how did you know?" The hotel is a big place.

"There are three groups that have pretty much

locked down all of the rooms in the hotel this weekend, and I don't think that you belong to the other two."

I'm offended by her assumption that I couldn't be with any other group in this hotel. What is she trying to say? Although I guess that's what people do. Make assumptions about others based on limited information. I suppose I did the same thing to her.

"I'm pretty sure your group went to the Galaxy Bar after dinner. That's the lounge on the seventh floor."

Dammit, I'm in the wrong place.

"Thanks," I say curtly.

When I motion to stand up from my stool, I feel loopy. Objects in the room are starting to wave and ripple, and suddenly I wish I was sitting on a chair that was a little lower to the ground and had a back to it.

I'm going down.

"Whoa there. Are you all right?"

Two very tall and wide masses of grinning flesh steady me by the waist, and gratefully I don't fall and split my head open.

"Thanks guys," I offer.

Both guys start cracking up.

"It was an easy save, Freshman. No problem."

"Why are you calling me that? I'm not in college anymore."

"Could have fooled me by the way that you drink."

"I just had a couple of drinks, Mr. Need To Mind Your Own Business. That goes for both of you."

"You're cute."

"You're blurry."

"Aww, you're really twisted aren't you?"

"Twisted?"

"Drunk."

"I don't think so. Wouldn't I be slurring?"

"You are slurring," one of them laughs.

Another blurry mass yells from across the room, "Hey, man. Next round is on you!"

"You and your friends are like gigantic. Look how they barely fit in the seats. I think they're going to break the couches over there," I giggle.

I can't stop laughing.

"You want another drink, Freshman?"

I may be tipsy, but I'm not stupid.

"So you can have some sort of ménage with me? Uh, I think not." I frown.

That gets me a huge laugh.

"First of all there's only one of me standing in front of you right now, and secondly I like my women sober, so they can at least remember my name when they call it out. I just wanted to buy you a drink, because I'm celebrating and evidently I'm also paying for everyone's third round in here."

"Celebrating what?"

"I just got dumped."

I don't know why anyone would celebrate that. Hell, at this point I'm still trying to figure out why I still see two of him.

"So you're sure you're not a twin?"

"Damn, you're cute in your little corporate suit, but this is bad timing. I've officially sworn off women."

For a moment I feel woozy and when I dip a little to the left on my stool, he quickly places his enormous hands back around my waist and saves me from another near death experience.

"Did you eat today, Freshman?" he asks with concern.

I usually eat six little meals a day, but at this point I'm sure I've missed at least two of them. I didn't eat anything at the dinner tonight, so my stomach is probably empty. Maybe I didn't think this drinking alcohol thing completely through.

"I may have skipped a meal."

The big guy doesn't sit down but continues to

stand behind me, still holding me by the waist, and speaks closely by my ear. If I wasn't so tipsy, it would be very sexy.

No wait, it is sexy.

"These are the basic rules to getting shit-faced, Freshman. You listening?"

I nod my head silently.

"Good girl. All right, so you need to eat before you drink. That's very important. You should drink the same alcohol all night. No mixing vodka with tequila. No red cups ever. Even at an office party. Pace yourself with glasses of water in between drinks. And never drink alone. That only leads to trouble."

"I like rules," I say not even fully processing everything he's said. "Rules are good."

"I see that." Is what I think he murmurs in response.

The bartender interrupts us by asking my new bar mate for his order. I find it amusing that when she talks to blurry guy that she seems to crack a smile. At least I think that's what she's doing. She's baring teeth at least.

"Can I get you something?"

Oh my God, is she being flirty with them? I mean him.

"I'll have another of whatever is on tap and drunky over here will have a nice tall glass of ice water."

"Hey!" I protest being called a drunk as well as his choice of drink for me. "I don't like water."

"Drink it anyway. I want to stop holding you on this stool. I'm sick of standing."

Humph. "Fine."

He sits on the stool next to me, spreads his massive legs apart, and pulls my stool forward in between them while holding my hips to keep me steady.

"So tell me. What's got you so upset that you've taken to the bottle? It's obvious to the average idiot that you don't do this often if ever."

Something about the warm tequila flowing through my veins and the vibes that blurry guy gives off, gives me the courage to discuss my dismal love life. I'll never see this guy again, and there's a sliver of a chance that he could actually help, so I talk. It's hard though, because I have to make sure to focus on only one of them.

"There's a guy."

"Go on."

"He's here."

"Where?"

"In the hotel. We're on our annual retreat."

"Oh so you work with him?"

"Yes. He's new."

"Okay, and?"

I take a chug of my ice water. It's actually refreshing, because the alcohol has me practically sweating like a pig.

"And he doesn't know I exist."

"I find that hard to believe."

"It's true."

"That's why you're upset?"

"We were just in a dinner meeting before I came here. We were all doing team-building exercises. He didn't want to team up with me. I could tell. I might've said a few things to embarrass myself after that. Then I ran out."

"Paranoid much?"

"He either didn't want to team up with me, or I'm invisible to him."

"Are there a lot of other women on the team?"

"A few."

"Young like you?"

"Yeah."

"Well there you go. There are too many distractions for the poor guy. I know the feeling well. You're going to have to figure out how to get some one-on-one time with Mr. Clueless."

I squint my eyes. "Are you positive you don't have a twin brother?"

"No," he chuckles. "Do you still see two of me?"

He waves his hand directly in front of my face.

"Yes," I say emphatically. "And you both have identical black eyes."

"Drink more water. When the good Lord made me, he broke the mold. So I guarantee that you should only be seeing one of me as well as one black eye courtesy of my brother over there."

I take another big gulp of my water.

"Why should I take your dating advice anyway? You just got dumped."

"The reason why you should take advice from me is because it works. It's how my bitch of an ex snagged me. She made sure to get my attention first, and then went in for the kill."

"Why did she dump you?"

"I have no idea."

"You should go after her."

"I started to, but then I changed my mind."

"If you loved her, you would have gone after her."

"Love shouldn't take that much work, Freshman."

"Maybe you weren't romantic enough. Women love romance."

"Who needs romance when she has *this* to wake up to every morning."

"The two of you think very highly of yourselves."

"Still seeing double huh," he snickers. "I think you better call it a night, Freshman."

"I was on my way to the seventh floor. I don't want to just go to bed without saying something to him. I ran out of the room like a complete moron today."

"Can I be honest with you?"

"You mean you weren't honest before?"

"Men are dumb, but we ain't stupid. Trust me when I say that he knows exactly who you are already, and if he were the least bit interested he'd have his eyes on you right now. He'd be in this bar right now. The fact that he isn't here tells me that he's not the guy for you."

"He should be chasing me but you shouldn't be chasing your fiancée?"

"Exactly."

"I think you're wrong. He's the perfect guy for me."

"There's no such thing, Freshman. My parents come damn near close to the perfect couple, and they still have their issues. There is no perfect guy. Only the right guy."

His words are starting to fade, as I try to keep my eyes open. I am ten seconds away from sprawling out on this floor and catching a nap.

"I'm *soooo* sleepy."

"What room are you in?"

"I dunno. 342 or maybe 324."

He laughs at my confusion and the next thing I know I'm seven feet in the air.

"Wait–"

"Quiet. I'm making sure you get to your room safely. My cousin Ben is starting to give you the hungry eye over there."

"The hungry eye?"

"Yeah, like he wants to eat you for dessert. Literally."

Uh-oh.

"Where's your key card?"

"My suit pocket. Just make sure he doesn't see me like this."

"Who, my cousin?"

"No, Jason, the new guy." I say drowsily.

I do my best to keep my eyelids open in case I need to cry for help. I'm breaking all of my personal safety protocols by allowing a complete stranger to carry me in an elevator and up to my room; but I'm no match for the deep sleep that the alcohol is placing me under, although I stay alert just long enough to hear a garbled promise that I hope is kept.

"Don't worry, Freshman. I've got you."

CHAPTER FOUR

SAINT

Sweat and salt dripping down my blazing hot back.

Chunks of the earth underneath my fingernails.

The gritty taste and texture of fresh turf in-between my teeth.

Football is what I eat, shit, and breathe.

I've been playing the game my entire life, and I've played with sprained ankles, broken ribs, jammed fingers, sore Achilles tendons, and black eyes; but the one thing that I've never gotten used to is tossing the ball around in ninety degree heat with a helmet and pads on. I hate that shit. I'd rather play in the snow any day.

I come from a lineage of professional football players. Football royalty is what they call us. The Stevenson Family. My father played the game. My uncle. My cousin. My older brother currently plays in the league, and so do I. I'm sure if I have any sons, they'll be expected to play as well. It's what we love. It's what we do. It's who we are.

Every fall as a kid I played football for my high school, but every summer it was a requirement that my brother Michael and I play in our family's football camp a.k.a. our summer league for kids with high football IQs and professional potential. It's called the Stevenson Summer Combine and it's a big deal. Any kid who doesn't play football for a highly visible high school program wants to come to our camp to hopefully be noticed by scouts. Our family is well connected, but it's no picnic. We played all day, everyday, and every summer at that camp whether we wanted to or not. Whether we'd rather be riding bikes or eating water ice because it was so hot. It was our duty as Stevensons to be there.

Football is our legacy.

In those days we played on some of the hottest, humid Philadelphia summer mornings straight through to the late afternoons. I remember feeling many times like I was going to keel over and pass out. Luckily my older brother Michael knew when I was about to eat rocks, and made sure to pour a pint of Gatorade down my throat, before I met my maker.

That's exactly the same way I feel now. Blazing hot, and a bit nauseous, but I can't totally blame the heat for it. If I'm going to be totally honest, I haven't been sticking to my usual clean diet of protein and veggies. I ate crap and drank more beer than I should've last night, because I felt like wallowing. Hell, I deserve to wallow. I'm in a miserable situation.

Last year my team, The New York Nighthawks, finished second to last place in the league. The year before that we were dead last. The year before that? Hell, I don't even like to think about my rookie year. We sucked balls. And right this very minute, we don't look any fucking better than we did last season. Which is nuts because ...

I'm the franchise player.

The star.

I put butts in the seats and pay the bills around here. So why is my team complete trash? I'll tell you why. I don't have any support. I'm getting my ass kicked out here week after week, and nobody in the head office is doing anything about it. It doesn't take a rocket scientist to diagnose what the problem is. I see it. My father sees it. The fans see it too.

Management needs to concentrate on working the kinks out of my offensive line. Unfortunately to stay well under the team's salary cap, our penny pinching owner has secured all these wet behind the ear rookies or broken down veterans that the coaching staff seems to be struggling to put in place to protect me out there on the field. It's even more critical now because we've finished the pre-game season, and now we're about to enter into the regular season, and they *still* don't have it figured out.

Unfortunately that's always been the biggest problem here in New York. Finding the right players at the right price point to protect me every Sunday, because I get sacked more than any other quarterback in the league, and that shit is no fun. When commentators throw out my stats in a broadcast it sounds as if I'm the worst quarterback to have ever played the game, and that I don't know my ass from my elbow. But that's far from the truth.

I'm the shit.

I was the number one draft pick.

I won the Heisman Trophy.

I've been raised to dominate and to win. So I definitely know how to avoid my opponents when I'm on the field, but the fact remains that I need time to throw the ball. It's that simple. Football 101. You can't blame me if management can't do their jobs, and pay five good men more money then they've ever seen in their lives to protect me and give me time to throw the damn ball.

"Stevenson!"

"Yes, coach."

"Meet the new guy. We're putting him in place of Wachowski."

That's just great. Ten minutes ago my tight end got trampled, and the backup is suspended because of a drug violation; so now after halftime, I'm going to be thrown in the middle of the goddamn game with a tight end I've never met before.

I realize that injuries and last minute replacement of players is part of the game, but I still hate that shit. I'm having a hard enough time establishing chemistry with the players that I already know.

"Pleasure, man," the new guy says eagerly.

I reluctantly shake hands with this big ass, grinning, muscle-head who appears to be my new tight end. I don't feel like meeting this kid right now, because we're losing and I'm pissed. Plus I don't feel like making pleasantries, or getting friendly with new players. He may not make the cut. Then I've gotten all attached for nothing. I learned that hard lesson my rookie year in the league. Nobody's job is safe. Everyone is expendable.

"What's up," is all I mange to say in response.

I'm not trying to have a full blown conversation with the new kid, when we only have a few minutes to figure out how the hell we're going to get the ball into the end zone next quarter.

"Followed you when you played for Capitol City, man. I'm a real fan."

"Thanks."

I don't really like talking about my time at my alma mater, Capital City College. Mainly because I was a winner there. A *phenom* as the papers often described me. And people often compare my performance there to my performance now. Which can be best described as *not* winning.

"Cooper's got the goods," Coach says with confidence. That's unusual for him to speak so highly of someone who's brand spanking new to the team, but I've been sold the same bullshit before. So I'm not going to even get my hopes up.

"Excellent," I respond with faux enthusiasm. "We need someone on this team besides myself who has *the goods.*"

"Looking forward to helping out," Cooper says then he walks away towards the rest of the team who's waiting to hear our usual halftime strategy slash pep talk. I say *usual* because it seems like we're always losing after the second quarter, and therefore always getting these types of motivational speeches.

Yet that shit never seems to work.

I pause for a moment to myself, thinking that I may have come off as a bit of an arrogant asshole to the new guy, but he'll just have to understand. It's just my frustration talking. The press has been ripping me a new one over the last two seasons and it's been taking its toll.

I feel the weight of each and every season on my back and it's heavy like a motherfucker. When we lose, and we lose a lot, everyone looks at me as if this shit is not a team sport. As if it's all on me. They say I don't protect the ball. That my arm is not as powerful or accurate as it used to be. They say I don't play like I want to win. As if I don't want a championship ring when that's all I want. It's all I've ever wanted. It just seems so far out of my grasp right now. I can't seem to see a bright light at the end of this loserville tunnel.

"Stevenson!"

"Yes, Coach." I answer one of my other coaches - Coach B.

"We have plenty of time to turn this thing around. Stop trying to go for the damn touchdown every throw. Just get a first down for Christ's sake!"

"Somebody needs to catch or run the damn ball in order for me to do that, Coach B." I say loudly enough for all of my sloppy wide receivers to hear.

"*Somebody* will if you'd just throw it to the man you're supposed to. We've run these plays all week, but you seem to have forgotten every single one," Coach B replies icily.

The team's offensive coordinator, Coach Benny, is not my biggest fan. Rumor has it that he actually wanted to go with the number two quarterback in the draft the year I entered instead of me. As a matter of fact, I was told the owner didn't particularly want me that badly either, although he'd never admit to that publicly.

From what I can tell over the last three years that I've been with the Nighthawks, only our head coach, Coach Ryan, really wants me here. That's why I try my best to work my ass off for him, as well as for myself. I don't ever want his position to be in jeopardy because of me, but clearly I'm not doing such a good job of that, because after halftime, we lose by seven points.

A-fucking-gain.

CHAPTER FIVE

SAINT

I don't even bother showering right after the end of the game, because I refuse to get cleaned up to go face the firing squad of reporters. So I just wipe the sweat off of my body with a towel, toss on one of my signature gold Nighthawk hoodies, lift the hood up to make sure it covers my entire head, and walk into the press room.

I really wish I could wear my shades, so they can't start making shit up about what my facial expressions say about my state of mind, but the team will probably try to fine me if I do that. So I compromise by only wearing the hoodie.

The questions start flying from all over the room, and like usual I answer only the ones I want. The way I want.

"Saint, what did you say to your teammates during halftime to try and get their heads back into the game?"

"Whatever I said didn't work, now did it?"

Next.

"Saint, how do you feel about Wachowski's injury?"

Fucking Annoyed. That jerk can't stay healthy to save his life.

"Disappointed."

Next.

"Saint, what do think about some of the official's questionable calls today?"

"They were bullshit."

Next.

"Saint, over here! Do you think you'll make the playoffs this year?"

A random reporter asks this stupid question. I've never seen him in the pit before. He's probably some sort of lame ass sports blogger. He looks all of eighteen years old. I guess the league gives anyone a press pass nowadays.

So Stupid.

"We gotta win at least one game first," I reply in a smart aleck voice.

Next.

"Saint, what do you think you need to do to turn things around this season?"

Now this guy I know. Jim Mathers. He's practically a relic. An old, balding guy from The Football Network, and he always asks the same irritating questions. Every single game.

"Score," I deadpan.

Next.

"Saint, unlike you, your brother seems to be having a fantastic start to his season in Seattle. How do you feel about that?"

And that question comes from a reporter named Myra Kitch. Rhymes with bitch. She's the worst out of the bunch. She's had it in for me since the day the Nighthawks signed me. She probably would play football herself if they allowed women to play in the pros. She's bigger and rougher than half of my offensive line, but because she's a woman, I have to be *extra careful* with how I handle her.

The team's PR people have repeatedly warned me that I need to be careful and make sure to keep my statements politically appropriate. That shit infuriates me though. Where's the equality in that? I should be able to rip her a new one like I do any male reporter when they ask me something asinine.

"That's a stupid question, Myra," I respond. Because it is.

"Is it? The way I heard it you Stevensons are highly competitive, and that you might not be so happy about your brother's success."

What the fuck is she talking about?

"You heard wrong." Myra Kitch the She-bitch.

No one has ever dared pit the two Stevenson brothers against each other like she's doing. We're America's football family. Hell, they had my mother on Good Morning America teaching Robin Roberts how to bake the perfect apple turnover and dancing to a live performance by Brad Paisley.

No one but this woman, this very evil woman, with a wider neck than my great-grandmother Stevenson (and that was one big woman), would make it seem as if me and Mikey are jealous of each other's success when that could be the furthest thing from the truth.

My dad's probably cringing right now as he watches me lose some of my composure on national television. He always taught me to be humble and smile when on camera, but I'm not in the mood for either of those things. I can't stand this part of the game. Whoever the hell came up with the idea to interview players ten minutes after they've put their asses on the line for four quarters and come up short was either an idiot or a sadistic genius. No player or coach wants to talk to the press after a loss. No one wants salt poured into their wounds when they've just been sliced and diced for the nation to see.

I can't wait for the day when I get to silence these jerks. The day that I finally get my championship ring. They'll all be kissing my ass when that day comes, because that's all you really have to do to shut reporters up. To shut everyone up.

Is win.

After wasting thirty minutes of my life in a press conference, I try scrubbing the layer of "loser" off of me in the shower, and when I'm finished I'm not surprised to see that I have a visitor waiting for me at the entrance of the locker room.

I always do.

This one is dressed in very little clothing, has the best tits her money can buy, legs for days, and is staring at me like I'm the answer to all of her problems. I'm not even going to bother asking security how she got all the way through to the player's locker room. A supposedly secure area.

All I have to do is take a look at how her huge *National Geographic* looking nipples are practically poking through her clingy Red Bull tank top to know. She's one of *those* girls. The kind that would step over just about anybody to get what she wants, and today what she wants seems to be me.

Typically a visit from a woman like this would be just the kind of escape I'm looking for after an abysmal game like today and a press conference like the one I just had.

They basically line up for us after the games. Cleat chasers. Ball groupies. Normally one will give me a blow job in the car, and if she knocks that out of the park, then maybe I give her a quick fifteen minutes of banging her from behind back at her place. That's all I usually want from girls like her, but I'm guessing by her body language that is what she wants too.

It's what they all want

Quick and dirty. Something to brag to their girlfriends about. Sex with the Gunslinger. Sex that their delusional asses are hoping will spoil it for all the other women after them, so that I'll come back specifically to them for more. But what this woman doesn't understand, just like all the women before her, is that there is no pussy in the world that will make me give up all the others. Forget all the others? That's never going to happen. I'm not built like that. Not anymore.

I've been getting pussy thrown at me since I was damn near fourteen years old. I guess because playing football is like catnip for certain women, case in point, this one standing in front of me licking her lips is a prime example.

Yet for some reason I can't explain my dick isn't jumping at her blatant offer. All I can seem to think about is the straight-laced, uppity woman, wearing the tight pencil skirt and bad attitude, with curves for miles from the restaurant the other night.

The girl who has no idea who I am.

Who doesn't remember me at all.

Twenty-four hours before I met her that first time, I had just been dumped by my fiancée Adrianna. Even though I trashed one of the rooms of the hotel, management was understanding. First of all the wedding was paid for, all my childhood friends and family were in town, and I'm kind of a celebrity.

So we decided to stay and we spent the rest of my wedding weekend getting fucked up.

I noticed her the minute I walked into the bar that night. She was throwing back tequila shots and wobbling around on her stool with little grace but boundless beauty.

I listened to her sob story about liking some loser at her job, and then I gallantly tucked her into her hotel room bed without even as much as a peck on the cheek.

It's been a few days since our second meeting, but I still have her business card lying in the center console of my car, and I have no explanation for why I haven't tossed it or used it. In fact, all I've been doing is reading it over and over, and adjusting the hard-on between my legs every time I do.

Sabrina White.
Junior Account Manager, Carson Financial.
Midtown Manhattan.
212-555-5484

. . .

"You need a *ride* somewhere, Gunslinger?"

The groupie's provocative questioning snaps me out of my train of thought like a splash of cold water.

"Nah, I've got a ride."

"Then how about I take your mind off of things and onto better things while you take that ride."

Quick and dirty girl makes her move in a tone full of sexual promise, but one I'm not really in the mood for. Usually, I rely on noncommittal girls like her to make me come hard and snap me out of the funk a bad game puts me in.

But not tonight.

The groupie and her Red Bull tank top remind me of something. I'm Saint fucking Stevenson and bad season or not, I should at least have endorsements flying out of my ass, and I know just the girl that can get them for me.

CHAPTER SIX

SABRINA

I notice it immediately. The office feels transformed the moment I walk off the elevator and into the main foyer. While Mondays are my favorite day of the week, they typically aren't anyone else's at my workplace. Yet today there seems to be a vibrancy floating through the air and bouncing around from person to person.

Contained excitement.

Reserved glee.

I'm not sure that I can explain it. Everything *seems* normal. My coworkers are at their cubicles with fresh lattes and small Pyrex bowls of warm oatmeal, typing away, writing on sticky notes, or texting on their cell phones about one thing or another. But something is definitely different, and I can't quite put my finger on what it is. Whatever's going on, I'm clearly the last person to know. I just hope it's a sign that I'm going to have a good mid-year evaluation.

"Morning, Sabrina"

"Morning, Peter."

It's common at the company for employees at my level of junior management to have mid and final year reviews with a supervisor and a senior level account manager both present in the room. In my case today that's my team supervisor Peter and my friend who's a senior account manager, Marisol.

"So before we get into the thick of your review, Sabrina, we wanted to talk to you about some changes that are happening within the company. Exciting changes."

My eyes widen. Oh my God, is Peter going to give me Spin? Marisol silently nods her head back and forth behind Peter's back as if she can read my mind.

Spin is one of Carson Financial's top clients. They are an award-winning, platinum-selling band, that sells out stadiums every time they tour. Their account manager Priscilla Carson just left the company after finding out her husband, and Carson Financial founder, has been having a long-standing affair with his executive assistant. So now Spin is abruptly without a full-time money manager, and the company needs to fill the spot quickly, before the group walks away from us completely and takes their money with them.

It's no secret at my office that there is only room for one new senior account manager to join the fold, and that both my coworker (and frenemy) Abby and I want the position. If one of us is assigned the Spin account, that will speak volumes about who's going to get the promotion. It means that we're trusted with a Tier-One, A-level client. Opportunities typically offered to only senior level or rising senior managers. For me it's a serious long shot, because I'm so young. Abby has seniority, but I truly believe I work twice as hard as she does.

"So it's just come down from the powers that be that Carson is expanding our brand. No longer will we be limited to musical entertainers, but we've now opened our doors to professional athletes. In fact, there is an entire new division of the company under development. The Carson Athletic division."

My supervisor Peter sounds almost excited as a kid on Christmas morning as he talks about this big expansion the company's making. And I get it. Athletes make tremendous amounts of money and have huge international profiles. What's not to like ... if you're management. If you're Peter. But this isn't the direction I'd hoped this conversation was going to go.

Now I'm starting to understand the silent head nod from Marisol. She knew I wasn't getting Spin or getting the promotion I was hoping for at all. She also knows how much I hate sports and despise professional athletes. They're just overgrown kids who get paid way more money than anyone should be allowed to earn for kicking or hitting a ball. I've never been able to understand that concept ever since I was a kid.

"We're starting off small. The Downtown office is getting three players. I think two of them are baseball and one is tennis, and our office is getting three new clients as well. One of them I feel very confident about giving to you, Sabrina. Best of all he's a football player."

Best of all?

"They call your new client The Gunslinger. Ring any bells?" Peter asks excitedly.

I think I'm supposed to have heard of this guy but I haven't.

"Umm, not really."

Peter chuckles, "That's all right. Marisol mentioned that you don't really follow sports. So maybe I'll have Jason help get you up to speed. He worked with ball players at his previous company. Is that okay with you?"

I'm a little shell shocked, but I go ahead and nod yes. Marisol grins like she always does whenever Jason's name is mentioned. I swear she's going to get me to the altar and popping out Jason's babies even if it kills her. She's worse than my mother, albeit a little more optimistic about getting me married.

"The only important things to know for now are that he's the franchise quarterback for the New York Nighthawks, he's being paid the rookie wage cap of twenty-two and a half million for four years, and he's never signed with a money manager before. His father has been taking care of his investments."

It's quiet for a moment in the room until Marisol breaks the silence with a loud clap. "That's a fantastic client, Sabrina! Congratulations, girl," she says with a little extra added enthusiasm in her voice.

I guess she can tell by the look on my face that I'm completely overwhelmed by Peter's news and maybe a little freaked out. I know zilch about football.

"That's right, Sabrina," Peter chimes in. "The company is giving you this account and with it is expressing pretty much everything that I planned on verbalizing in today's mid-year review. You are an excellent account manager. You have the type of work ethic and attention to detail that Carson Financial values. You've met all of your goals last quarter, and more importantly we value you as a person.

"Good work and congratulations," Peter commends as he hands me a plain manila folder with a stapled packet inside.

"The Gunslinger's one sheet is in here along with a portfolio of his current assets. His game and practice schedule is grueling, so unfortunately the only time he has over the next two weeks to meet with you and sign his paperwork is later today at four o'clock.

"When you meet with him, make sure to have him sign the contract and discuss how things work with us. I've come up with a few goals that you can discuss, which I'll email you, since I know you weren't prepared for all of this today, but feel free to run with any ideas you may come up with.

"I'm giving you full rein with this client, but obviously we'll be watching you closely. He's pretty important to us. So make sure you document things well. Add all significant meetings to the calendar. And just do what you do. Making sure to leave a paper trail that management can check if need be."

I accept the folder reservedly, while my brain is moving a mile a minute. Change is difficult for me. It builds a level of anxiety within me that I am working very hard to keep at bay this very minute. A trait passed down to me from my wonderful nervous Nellie of a mother.

Signs that my nerves are frayed? Well, right now I am dying for a bag of potato chips and a Pepsi, and it's only nine in the morning. Grease and sugar cravings are a sure giveaway that I'm spiraling.

I'm dying to ask Peter why the hell he gave *me*, of all people, this particular client. *Is this some sort of test?* I want to yell at Marisol and tell her to stop laughing at me with her eyes, because trust me, she's cracking up at the fact that I'm silently unraveling. And most of all, I want to smack myself for being so ungrateful. While any sane person would look at this meeting as a sign that their career trajectory is on the right track, and be jumping up and down with excitement, all I can seem to dwell on are all the things that could go wrong, very wrong.

Number one. Carson Financial is known for its

management of music entertainers. That is what we specialize in. That is where most of the managers' passions lie (such as myself), and it is where most of our connections are, with companies that want to do business with music entertainers. We (I) don't know the first thing about athletes.

Number two. I don't like sports. I don't watch football, baseball, soccer, hockey, or tennis. I don't even watch the Olympics. Winter or summer. And when the sports segment comes on the evening news, I turn the sound down and read a book. Some of my attitude might have to do with the fact that I suck at sports, some of it might have to do with a little crush I had on a very evil baseball player in high school, but mostly it has to do with the fact that I have a big problem with grown men being overpaid to do what they've been doing since they were three years old ... play. Imagine someone paying me millions of dollars to play Words With Friends on my cell phone? Now that would be freakin' awesome.

Number three. I don't want any new accounts distracting me from my real mission. Becoming a senior account manager. There's no doubt that this ball player is probably young, dumb and has more money than he knows what to do with; how on earth am I going to impress management when I'm going to be stuck with such an unpredictable client. If they would just give me Spin, this would be so easy.

I just love their story. Three high school friends, determined not to sell out, writing socially conscious music in their garage, determined to share their art with the world. Doing a lot of pop-up shows for free, so that all their fans have the opportunity to see them live. And the lead singer Marley. On top of the fact that he's gorgeous, the texture and tone of his voice is haunting and makes you feel like he's singing directly to you. About you. For you.

I'm a numbers girl, and I don't have an artistic bone in my body, so I really respect people who have the gift to create art like that and are brave enough to share it with the world. Not to mention that they make a ton of money at it, and from what Marisol has told me about them, they not only make great money but they spend it wisely. They often give a lot of it away to meaningful charities. Never seeking any press or recognition for their good deeds. Who on earth wouldn't want to have them as a client? Who wouldn't look good with them on their roster?

Ugh, I can feel my nerves churning inside of my stomach like a mixture of bad barbecue and warm beer. This is so off my plan. A huge detour. I have to become a senior manager in the next twelve to eighteen months if I want to stay on track. If I don't, then I'm going to have to re-evaluate my plan, which I really don't want to do. Because like I said, I hate change.

But if this is some sort of test from management, then perhaps I need to look at this whole thing differently. Maybe try altering my way of thinking. This could be a massive opportunity for me if I handle things correctly. Make the most out of it. Bide my time. And then I'm sure I'll get what I deserve eventually. I've got good people in my corner like Marisol and Jason. Yeah, I'm just going to have to bide my time.

"Thank you so much, Peter. I know that this is an amazing opportunity, and I'm honored that you've offered it to me."

"You've earned it, kid. Remember four p.m. in the small conference room. I'll have Dawn order a platter or something and put it in there. You like Pepsi right?"

"Yes, but make it diet," I say brightly. Surprised that he remembers such an irrelevant piece of trivia about me. But I guess that's why he's the boss. He is excellent with small details, and he knows how to make everyone feel special.

"And that, my friend, brings your mid-year evaluation to a close." Marisol throws her arm around my shoulders.

"Any questions about the account can be directed to me or your mentor Jason." She winks.

"Great." I smile. "Thank you, both."

Peter gets up to leave first, and as soon as the door closes behind him, I snap my head around to Marisol in an almost panic. She throws her hand up to stop me before I can even blurt anything out first.

"Stop it. I know what you're going to say. You still want Spin. You hate sports. You don't think that you can do this. But trust me when I say that they wouldn't give you a twenty-two million dollar client if they didn't have plans on making you a senior level manager very soon. Also, look at it this way, it's the perfect excuse for you to work with Jason even more. He is the only senior level here with experience working with athletes."

"Then why on earth didn't they give him the account?"

"He's getting one of the other ones."

"This makes absolutely zero sense."

"Just think about all the legitimate reasons you'll have to ask for a consultation with him." Marisol grins.

"You do realize that you are not a professional

matchmaker don't you? This is my career we're talking about. Plus, I don't want to marry the guy. I just have a little crush."

"Little?! I think you need to remember who you're talking to. You've had eyes for him ever since he started working here three years ago. That's a long ass crush."

"It's not like I'm waiting around for him. I've dated other people."

"I realize you have needs and that you've seen a few guys here and there, but let's not forget that I know that he's the one you really want. And I'm all for it. You just have to let go of the whole retreat thing and open up. Allow him to see the real you. Not just the persona you display here at work."

"There's a bigger problem than my love life right now, Marisol. I have a meeting with the star player of a professional football team, and I don't even know that I've ever seen an entire football game in my life."

"That's okay. You're his financial manager not his coach."

"I know music, not sports."

"You know money, and you'll learn whatever you need to about sports. Do I need to reiterate how much money he makes? Don't dismiss this opportunity, Sabrina.

"There are just a few things I need to warn you about though. This guy's family is football royalty, and they're very close knit. They don't do outside people well at all. So expect some push back from his camp."

"All right and what else?"

"The other thing is that this Stevenson guy is like a rock star on steroids. Drop dead hot. Obviously loaded. He parties hard and runs through women like crazy. And he's probably an ass. He was seen at Wimbledon last summer saying something in his date's ear to make her cry. Cameras caught it."

"Wimbledon?"

"Tennis, Sabrina. It's the name of the tennis championship held in England every year. You must know about that?"

"Of course I've heard of that." Barely. "Celebrities go to that?"

"Big ones," she answers, as if she's exhausted by my sports ignorance.

"Okay, but what's your point?"

"He's charming to say the least, and let's call a spade a spade, you're vulnerable. So just stay professional. Don't let him get under your skin or inside your panties."

"You're kidding right?"

"I know who I'm talking to. I realize you have zero interest in pro athletes. Especially womanizers like him, but as a fellow woman, I felt like I should at least warn you. Stronger women have fallen under the spell of men just like him."

"Your warning has been duly noted, but trust me when I say that you have nothing to worry about. I have a very friendly electronic boyfriend at home that takes care of the cobwebs in between fellas."

"Don't we all."

We both cackle.

"So does the office know about this guy already? I mean everyone's been acting weird this morning."

"Well the team did get an email about the new sports division, but not about Stevenson specifically. Peter may have conveniently taken your name off of the email distribution list. He wanted you to be surprised. He was actually very excited to give this client to you. He really thinks you have senior level potential. He's pushing for you, Sabrina. So this Gunslinger guy is your Spin. Make it work."

I seriously doubt that, but I guess stranger things have happened.

As I make my way back to my cubical, I start getting a few "happy eyes" from coworkers.

They know.

Not just about the new sports division, but it's obvious that they know that I have one of the clients in that new department.

I try to graciously smile in acknowledgement of everyone's stares, and then I sit down at my cubicle and take a look at my computer screen.

I shake the mouse to stop the screen saver and check my inbox. Sure enough Peter sent another email about five minutes ago announcing the managers who will handle the three clients of the newly created Carson Financial sports division: Jason Humphrey, Samuel Parson, and myself. Out of us three, I am the only junior level manager, which means that this is definitely a big deal for me.

Perhaps Marisol is right. Maybe this is my gateway to becoming a senior manager. All right then, Mr. Gunslinger, let's learn more about you...

I pull my packet out which has the one sheet on top and can't believe my eyes when I see his photograph.

Client: Saint Stevenson a.k.a. The Gunslinger
Height: 6' 5"

Weight: 245 lbs
Position: Quarterback
Team: New York Nighthawks
Current Season: Fourth
Contract Terms: Four years; 22.5 million.
Endorsements: Lucky Sports

It's him.

Those titanium eyes.

That strong jaw.

The man who touched me and damn near set me on fire.

The man I made kind of a fool of myself in front of, because I didn't think I'd ever see him again.

The man I'm going to see and sign to a contract in less than seven hours.

Oh my hell.

CHAPTER SEVEN

SABRINA

I'm a rule player, not a rule breaker. It makes life simpler when everyone's clear on what the rules are, what people's expectations are of you, and then you just follow that blueprint. But today I'm not going to follow the unwritten rule of working through lunch, like I usually do. In fact, today I'm going to go to an actual restaurant for an entire hour and make sure to order an alcoholic beverage while I'm there. Like a total rebel!

I've got a meeting this afternoon with a man I had no intentions of ever seeing again. A man I verbally sparred with. Flirted with at the end. A man I'm obviously and inexplicably attracted to. A man that knows I'm attracted to him.

Oh my God, how on earth am I going to be able to work for this guy? How will he even be able to take me seriously?

Now my head is spinning. I understand so much more. Him wearing the ridiculous sunglasses at night. His spectacular body. The security guards. His complete arrogance.

He's a professional athlete.

A good one.

And now I've got to try and come up with some plausible reason why I can't take him on. A reason that won't get me stuck at junior management for the next ten years of my life or worse fired. And on top of all of that the only thing that could make this day worse has happened. Abby just walked in.

"Hi, Sabrina."

"Hey, Abby," I say with little enthusiasm hoping she'll get the hint to move on.

"What are you doing here? You usually work at your desk through lunch," she inquires as she judgmentally inspects everything on the table.

My phone (which is off). My choice of meal (I

ordered a shit load of carbs). My frozen alcoholic beverage (served in an obvious daiquiri glass).

"Just felt like taking myself out for lunch."

"Well congratulations. I read about you getting the football player."

She's so disingenuous. She's practically spitting nails.

"Have you heard of him?" I ask with a saccharin smile.

Abby gives me an incredulous look then sighs heavily as if she's about to teach the dumb girl a lesson.

"Of course I have. He's a huge star, Sabrina. He's like the second coming to the league. Everyone is looking for him to bring the city our first championship in over twenty-one years."

She places one of her pointy-nailed hands on her hip.

"Huh, I'm surprised Peter even gave you Saint Stevenson considering you know nothing about football. It's not like you've ever tried to hide the fact that you don't follow sports. It's just so odd."

Good grief. Is it that obvious to everybody who I work with that I don't like sports? Just because I don't participate in the various betting pools they always have going?

"It's not odd to me. I won't be teaching him how to catch a ball. I'll be managing his money."

I throw a few of Marisol's words back at Abby, but instead of what I'm saying making some sort of poignant point and shutting her up, Abby bursts out into laughter instead.

"He doesn't *catch* anything, silly. He's paid to throw the ball. That's what quarterbacks do. Throw the ball."

"Catch. Throw. It doesn't matter," I say slightly embarrassed. "My only job is to keep him out of bankruptcy court."

"Wow. You don't hold much regard for professional athletes do you? I think that you should perhaps have higher aspirations for your client's financial well-being other than keeping him out of trouble."

I didn't mean it like that. Dammit, this girl has the extraordinary ability to push all of my buttons.

"Thanks for your concern, Abby, but I've got it under control. I know what I'm doing or they wouldn't have given him to me."

"Okaaay," she says with exaggerated uncertainty in her irritating singsong voice.

I should have known she'd be pissed. Everything with her is a competition.

"Have you heard any news about Spin?" I ask trying to change the subject.

"May I sit?"

I rather you didn't.

"I'm almost finished with my lunch so–"

"That's okay. I'll just wait while you finish. I'm not ordering food or anything. Some of us have to watch what we eat."

I suppose she's referring to the alcohol and carbs on the table, and the fact that Abby is at least three sizes smaller than me.

"Some of us are happy with a little cushion," I say defending my broad childbearing hips and ample bottom.

"I guess *some* of us are."

I wonder if I'd get arrested for tossing this frozen strawberry daiquiri in her face. I'd be really tempted to do it if it didn't taste so damn good.

"So do you have any information on Spin or not?"

She smirks before speaking.

"Well I overheard a conversation Peter was having on the phone. He's still trying to convince them into staying. So I guess he's not going to assign them a manager yet, since he isn't even sure that they're still clients. He's still got some sweet-talking to do I suppose. Especially to Marley. From what I heard, he's the main one who wants to leave."

That's not good news.

"So when do you meet Saint Stevenson?" she asks.

Now we're getting to the real point of her inserting herself into my peaceful lunch today. She wants information. She always wants something.

"Today."

"You need any help? I can help you prepare. Maybe sit in on the meeting with you, so you don't make a complete fool of yourself when he starts talking football. I grew up with two brothers who played since pee wee league. I know a lot about the game."

She must have been drinking daiquiris too, because if she were in her right mind, she'd know that I'd never agree to that ridiculous offer. Her in the room at my first meeting? In any client meeting? So she can try to sabotage it. Hell to the no.

"I have Jason for that," I brag.

"Oh?"

"He's worked with pro athletes before. So he's advising me."

"Oh right, I do remember him telling me that the other night."

Abby is on my last nerve. She wants everything I want for no real reason other than because I want it. She wants the senior management position, but doesn't work nearly as hard as I do. She wants Spin, but doesn't even own any of their music. And then one day she must have bumped her head, woke up, and decided that she wanted Jason. She flirts with practically every man in the office, but with him it's so obvious that it's nauseating. Evidently the male ego feeds off of *obvious* though, because Jason seems to lap it right up.

"So ... I need to finish up my lunch and get ready for my meeting."

My subtle way of telling her to go the hell away.

"Good luck with that," she says with zero sincerity.

"Yep. Bye."

The frozen daiquiri I drank at lunch is doing wonders for my nerves. Must have been the top shelf rum I requested or the fact that I never drink. That's why one drink always does the job for me. It's settled me down enough to take a longer look at my file and do a little further Google research on one Mr. Saint Stevenson.

I knew there was something familiar about this guy. Seems like Saint Stevenson was a football prodigy. I must have heard of him over the years at some point. A talented kid from a famous football family who went on to become a star in college but apparently is flailing in the pros.

Explains a lot about the vibe he gives off. A sense of entitlement, with a touch of arrogance, and something to prove. I've seen it a million times with so many of our celebrity clients. Young, rich, bored and reckless.

The stage has been carefully set for my first meeting with the man they call The Gunslinger. Peter's assistant ordered a mixed hoagie tray and another tray of assorted fresh fruit, which are set up in the small conference room. Apparently this guy likes to eat.

The whiteboard and my laptop are ready for me to give a slide show presentation, and several printed materials on Carson Financial are on the table.

I've done my best to freshen up. Other than smoothing out my slightly wrinkled skirt with my hands, I've brushed my teeth in the bathroom, applied a fresh layer of blush and lipstick, and popped a mint in my mouth for good measure.

Kate, our bubbly receptionist, pops her head in with a wide grin spread across her face. "Sabrina, he's here! Should I send him back here? Are you ready for him?!"

Kate looks around the room as if she's double checking on its cleanliness or something. She's quite excited.

"I'm ready. Send him in."

"Oh hi, Jason." Kate turns her head.

"Hey, Jason," I say with surprise and a little too much brightness in my voice. I need to remember to turn it down a notch, if I don't want to appear desperate and obvious to him. I work really hard to appear as if I'm not plotting on him every single second of the day.

"I thought I'd sit in on your first meeting just in case you run into any snags." He smiles.

"Let me guess." I smile back. "Did Peter or Marisol send you in here?"

"They may have mentioned that it would be a good idea for me to drop by."

"The Carson tag team strikes again. So I take it that you've been debriefed on the fact that I'm sports illiterate and football dumb."

"Yes, I have been, but I have plans to change all of that."

"Really?"

I like the sound of that.

"Absolutely. That's what mentors do right? Instead of working dinners, I'm thinking we should have a few working game days instead. We catch a game, I explain what's going on, and then you will learn the landscape and who the major players are in no time."

"Sounds perfect!" I say, yet again too brightly.

I can't help it though. I'm excited about the possibility of us spending all that quality time together.

Kate returns to the door with my new client in tow.

"This way, Mr. Stevenson," she says as she directs him inside of the conference room. Her lips covered in a fresh coat of iridescent lip gloss, which has me wondering how she found time over the last sixty seconds to put it on. I'm seeing already how this man has an effect on women, and giving him a once over as he crosses the threshold reminds me why.

Good Lord.

Let's just say his stats don't do him justice.

I already knew that Saint Stevenson towers over most human beings on the planet, but he's also wider and even more muscular than I remembered. I think I read somewhere online that he's unusually big for a quarterback, which apparently adds to his value as a player.

He's dressed very casually in a dark gray sweat suit, white sneakers, and a New York Nighthawks baseball cap. The soft cotton fabric of his hoodie basically caressing every peak and valley of his rock hard upper body. His loose sweatpants not quite baggy enough to hide the large package between his legs.

Avert your eyes, Sabrina.

He's not wearing any ridiculous sunglasses this time (thank God), but the brim of his hat has been purposely bent and shaped into a curve that hides his eyes. Maybe they're bloodshot. From what I've heard about him, bloodshot eyes would confirm Marisol's description of him as a big partier.

I run my hands down the sides of my skirt hoping to dry my clammy palms. I'm starting to wish I had worn my oversized gray power pantsuit which hides my curves a lot better than this skirt because after our first encounter, I need him to take me seriously, and not just look at me as a piece of meat.

Hell–let me just rip off the Band-Aid and get to it.

"Hello, Mr. Stevenson." I say in my brightest professional voice. "It's a pleasure to have you on board at Carson Financial. You've made a wise decision for your career."

"Why are you talking like that?" he asks while taking a seat at the table.

"I'm sorry what did you say, Mr. Stevenson?"

His sentences are being muffled beneath the brim of his hat.

"I asked," he takes off his cap and stares me straight on, "Why are you talking to me like some corporate hack, and call me Saint please, Mr. Stevenson is my father."

I am almost too dumbfounded to respond. This is my first time seeing his complete face, uncovered and close up. He is the epitome of perfect imperfection.

A close shaved beard which compliments his hard angles.

A very crooked nose.

Wide bloodshot eyes with pools of steel in the center.

A slight cleft chin.

And a permanent scar across his upper lip.

It's a crime for someone to look this good without even trying, or it really should be one.

"Okay, Saint then." I almost exhale the words without breathing.

"And who's this?" Saint turns his head and stares directly at Jason, but I can tell by his tone that he remembers exactly who Jason is, and now the realization of all the things I said that night hits me like a ton of bricks.

I told him Jason was my date.

I told him a lot of things.

"Pleasure to meet you, Mr. Stevenson." Jason extends his hand to shake Saint's. "I'm Jason Humphrey, senior account manager here at Carson Financial. I'm sitting in on this meeting as Ms. White's point person."

He doesn't say anything in response to Jason's introduction, but rather turns his head back to me, slightly tilted, with a curious glint in his eye.

"You date coworkers, Miss White? Do you think that's wise?"

I tap my foot nervously as I quickly try to think of a way to clean this up.

Jason clears his throat. "I think you have it wrong, Mr. Stevenson. Sabrina and I are coworkers. Our relationship is purely professional."

"Oh?" He looks down at me with a huge grin. "Maybe I did have it wrong. Sorry about that."

He grabs one of the bottled waters on the table, twists it open, and takes a long swig. "But you know what, Jase?"

Oh God, who on earth calls people by a nickname without having some sort of relationship with them first? Condescending jerks do that's who.

"I think that Miss White and I will be fine on our own today. You don't mind do you? I want to get to know my new business manager without any distractions. Without any barriers."

That last statement sounded pretty dirty, but I suppose he can't help it. Everything that comes out of his mouth sounds like sex. At least if feels that way to me.

And Jason looks a bit taken aback by the sex god's blunt words. In fact, as long as I've known him, I think this is the first time that I've ever seen Jason look a little intimidated by another man. But it's understandable. Everything about Saint Stevenson is intimidating.

"It was requested that I sit in–"

"Should we call the head of this division in then? Uh, what's his name?" Saint snaps his fingers obnoxiously as if he's trying to remember Peter's name.

Boy this guy is a terrible actor *and* a bully.

"Peter," I say in a huff to end his shenanigans.

"Oh that's right–Peter."

"Uh no, Mr. Stevenson. That won't be necessary. Sabrina is one of the best account managers in this office. She can absolutely handle this meeting on her own. I was just trying to be helpful."

"Well if we need your help, I'll make sure she calls you back in."

Jason leans into me. Our shoulders touching. His mouth very close to my ear.

"You all right with this, Sabrina?" he whispers. Still sounding unsure about leaving me to deal with this rude new client of mine.

"I've totally got this. I promise," I assure him.

He smiles in return.

"Of course you do. Call me when you're done okay?"

"Will do."

"Pleasure, Mr. Stevenson."

"Likewise."

CHAPTER EIGHT

SABRINA

When the door slams shut, I immediately get to the heart of the matter. No need to beat around the bush. This is how you have to deal with guys like him.

I adjust my seat and cross my right leg over my left, which is no easy feat in this skirt, and look him square in the eyes.

"So let's talk real talk, Mr. Stevenson," I say to him in my best big girl voice.

"Real talk, huh? All right let's do it," he says excitedly, then he flashes me a thousand watt smile, which has probably dropped a thousand pairs of panties across the nation.

"It can't possibly be a coincidence that you've hired this company to handle your financial affairs. The company *I* work for."

"You seem pretty sure that I'm up to something, Miss White."

"Well–"

"You think a company looking to enter sports management in a big way wouldn't have approached someone like me a long time ago?"

I shuffle uncomfortably in my chair. Is this just a coincidence, and I've now put my foot in my mouth? Did I offend him?

"I guess that–"

"But let me stop you there, because you would also be correct," he cuts me off. "It's not a coincidence that I'm here."

"So you're saying that you hired Carson Financial, because I work here?" I ask still a little unsure of what I may actually be insinuating.

"That's right."

I almost choke on my own saliva.

"Why?"

"I don't know. Why did you tell me you were on a date with your 'point person' when we met?" he counters using air quotes when he says the words point person.

"I'm not sure what one thing has to do with the other, but you were being quite presumptuous with me in the restaurant. You didn't know if I was on a date or not. Lying seemed to be the easiest solution for shutting you down."

"Is that still the case?"

"Is what still the case?"

"That you're not dating your coworker, because he seems very interested in what's happening in this room right now. In fact, I'd bet a hundred dollars that he's standing right outside of this room right this very minute."

Saint's eyes drop to my thighs.

"I bet it's killing him that the door to this room is closed, that you're dressed in *this*, and that he has no idea what I'm saying to you or doing to you."

"Doing to me?" I repeat appalled and aroused.

He walks over to the seat closest to me and sits down. His massive body taking up not only the space around me, but it almost seems as if he's filling the entire room. Just the insinuation of Saint Stevenson *doing* anything to me makes me pause. I mean I'd have to be dead not to be drawn in by the raw sexual heat this man emits.

"Yes," he practically growls. "Doing to you."

"Listen, Mr. Stevenson–"

"We've been over this, love. The name is Saint."

"Saint. Look, I want to be perfectly clear here. I'm not sure what game you're playing, but I have very little interest in games or in you as a client at this point."

He pauses for a moment as if he's carefully thinking of a response to my very frank but honest statement, and then he just goes ahead and asks me a question which is totally off topic.

"Are those authentic Philadelphia hoagies over there or New York's lame version of a sub?"

"I don't know. I didn't order them," I say flatly.

"Oh did the cute girl who walked me back here order them?"

Ugh, this guy.

"I. Don't. Know." I reiterate strongly.

"I'm just asking, because I usually eat clean during the season. If I'm going to cheat, I might as well go with the good stuff."

"I'm sure they were ordered from a reputable place."

"An authentic Philadelphia hoagie in New York? I doubt it. But could you be a darling and hand me one of the turkey and cheese ones anyway?"

The nerve.

"I'm sorry but did you hear anything that I said?"

"Something about no playing games. No interest in me as a client. Blah, blah, blah."

"That's right. I'm not interested in taking on you or any other professional athlete as a client. Especially under these ... circumstances."

He saunters over to the hoagie tray.

"Guess I'll help myself then," he says as he grabs one chunk of hoagie. Which is funny to me, because I bet he could probably eat all ten of those chunks and burn them off by dinner.

"Listen, Miss White. I don't think you're fully aware of what's at stake here."

He adds some of the side fixings to his hoagie, grabs another bottle of water, and has a seat across from me this time.

"Enlighten me then."

"I am one of the highest paid rookies in the league. Without having been solicited, I personally called your office, talked to your boss for fifteen minutes, and then agreed to sign with Carson Financial for a year but only with the stipulation that *you* would be my account manager."

I audibly gasp.

This guy is insane.

"You're finally getting it now, are you?" He licks his lips after chewing a small bite of his sandwich.

"If you don't take me on as a client, then I'll take my business elsewhere. I certainly didn't sign here to end up with that guy you've been schoolgirl crushing on for years to manage my money. He doesn't look fun at all."

"You are out of your mind."

And how does he know I've liked Jason for years?

"That's what they tell me, darlin'."

What should I do right now? If this Gunslinger jerk leaves the company because of me, I can certainly forget about my promotion. I may even lose my job. But if I take him on as a client, then I don't know what I'm in store for. I have no idea what he's up to. I don't play games, and I don't even pretend to know how to.

"What exactly do you want from me, Mr. Stevenson?"

He uses his strong legs to roll the chair he's sitting in completely around to my side of the table then sighs heavily before speaking again.

"You're all business aren't you? It's killing you to call me by my first name no matter how many times I ask you to. And look, you have stress lines etched across your beautiful forehead from this conversation. This isn't supposed to be a tense transaction. This is supposed to be good news. I'm the client that's going to make you a star around here. Don't you want that?"

Of course I do, but at what cost? And what's in it for him?

"I have to say that I'm really confused as to why you've offered *me* this opportunity. We had a five minute exchange in a restaurant a couple weeks ago. You don't know me."

"You remind me of someone I once met." He grins.

"So that's the criteria you're using to make major business decisions?"

"There's just something about you I trust. Is that better?"

"Wasn't your family managing your money before? You don't trust them?"

"You're starting to hurt my feelings, Miss White. If you don't want to manage my twenty-two million just say the word."

"I don't want to manage your twenty-two million," I say defiantly.

"Gah!"

Saint slams his hand down on the table in what seems like part frustration and part amusement.

"I like you, Miss White, so I'm going to give you one more chance to answer correctly."

"What else do I need to say for you to understand? I'm *not* interested."

"What is this prejudice you have against me or is it with professional athletes in general? What jock broke your heart in college or was it high school?"

He's hitting a little too close to home, the arrogant baller.

"I had no interest in jocks then or now," I lie just a little. "I prefer musicians. I specifically selected this company to work at because we represent really great musicians, and call me crazy, but I want to *like* the people I work for."

"Ouch, that hurts," he chuckles. "You're cold blooded, Miss White, but I guess that's only going to work in my favor when you make the big endorsement deals for me."

"What endorsement deals? I'm only managing the books. Paying your bills."

"No, that's what you do for those reality show singers you represent. For me, you're going to go get some endorsement dollars. I'm big time, Miss White."

"That's not what I do."

"That's not what you're comfortable with. Two very different things."

"Don't you have a sports agent, Mr. Stevenson?"

"My uncle is my agent."

"But you still want me to do double the work? Manage the books and find you endorsement dollars. That's your uncle's job. I'm assuming he hasn't done much on your behalf."

"You should probably read over your contract, Miss White. Making me more money is definitely part of your job."

I can see that my comment about his uncle seemed to rub Saint the wrong way. I kind of like that I have wiped the smirk off of his face, even though this is one of the most unprofessional exchanges I've had with a client ever in my life.

"But as you well know, a sports agent typically handles your major deals."

"My uncle has my best interest at heart, and he'll negotiate my league contract next year, but it's difficult to get endorsement dollars when your team isn't playing well."

His heavy posture tells me all that I need to know. I've hit a sore spot, and I can't believe I'm thinking this, but I'm actually feeling a little bad for the millionaire.

"I'm sorry about that, but I don't know if I can do any more for you than your uncle. Maybe your team will have a better season this year and things will turn around."

"Have you watched us lately?"

"To be honest, Mr. Stevenson, I don't watch football. So I don't know much about The Nighthawks."

"Well that's going to have to change."

"A lot of things would have to change for this to work."

"So you're reconsidering?"

"If I'm going to become your business manager, then we'd have to keep things perfectly professional between us. That means I need total honesty from you, and there will be no flirting."

He suddenly fingers the hem of my skirt.

"Is that what we're doing? Flirting?" he teases in a voice that's heavy and thick.

I clear my throat.

"And no discussing Jason unless it's in reference to something purely professional," I demand.

"Professional," his deep voice echoes back.

Damn he's distracting.

That voice.

That body.

That face.

And that smell. A subtle mixture of natural elements: water, earth and musk. Smells expensive and also very distinct. It's a scent that lets every woman know for miles around that a man is in the vicinity. A real man that chops wood, scares away burglars, and nails you hard in the shower.

Oh dear God. I'm losing it.

"Yes."

"Like you and the short dude are strictly professional."

What is his obsession with Jason?

"Exactly like that," I respond exasperated.

"You seem to have a lot of conditions in regards to me paying you and your company to take care of all of my money."

"Let's not forget that I didn't ask for the job."

"Ungrateful little–"

"And it may seem like a lot of conditions to someone like you, but in the real world it's not."

He scoots his chair even closer to the table and closer to me. The castors on the bottom of his chair squeaking as if they're not used to someone as heavy as him putting them to work.

"Someone like me? Oh, so I don't live in the real world?"

"I worded that poorly," I thinly apologize. "I meant in the average person's world."

"You've got me there, Miss White, because I'm definitely far from fucking average."

I barely hold back a snicker in reaction to that arrogant comment.

"I have a condition of my own," he announces.

I look up and firmly hold his eyes with my own in anticipation of whatever this is.

"And what could that possibly be?"

"If you're going to manage my money, and make me more money, then I want you to learn all about what I do for a living."

"I think I know enough about football to manage your financial affairs."

"Do you? Because you didn't know who I was, darlin', and that's a sure sign that you don't know shit about the game.

"I *am* football."

CHAPTER NINE

SABRINA

I've mopped my kitchen floor (if you can really call it mopping) with one of those hands-free wringing mops for the third time today. Every time I come back inside my tiny kitchen to check on the hot wings, which are warming in the oven, I see a new scuff mark that the legs of my counter stools have made across the floor, and so I mop yet again.

Obviously it's my nerves getting the best of me. Jason is coming over to watch the game and to begin giving me my lessons on the basics of football. The fact that he will be my tutor and inside my house makes learning about it much more bearable.

When my phone vibrates across my granite counter I know who it is. Very much like me, Jason is prompt. I'm pretty sure it's him calling to let me know that he's on his way. He's supposed to be here in about thirty minutes.

"Hello?"

"Hey Sabrina, I'm outside. I came a little early, so we can watch some of the pregame coverage."

What! I'm showered, but I'm dressed in my ratty Spin T-shirt and a pair of baggy sweats. I'm not wearing any make up, and I still have to empty this bucket of dirty mop water.

"Can you give me a few minutes?"

"I'll watch the pregame show while you finish doing whatever you're doing. Don't worry about me. I'll stay out of your way. Is it okay to park the car across the street in this neighborhood?"

Ugh, I guess I can't leave him sitting in his car. That would be seriously rude on my part.

"Umm, your car will be fine across the street. You can park there all day on Sundays. Alternate street parking is only during the week."

"Actually I was asking if it's safe. Have there been any break-ins in this area lately?"

Okay, I feel some kind of way about that comment, but I'm going to let it go. I realize that Jason lives in a more upscale neighborhood than I do, and that many people make assumptions about the safety of Brooklyn. As if it's still stuck in a crime ridden 1980s time warp. I just thought he was smarter than that.

"Not that I'm aware of. I'll unlock the front door for you because I have to run into the back for a moment. Let yourself in."

"Will do."

I live in a small garden floor apartment of a brownstone house in Brooklyn, New York. It's a revitalized neighborhood which is close to the Brooklyn Bridge, so it takes me only about thirty minutes to get to work, which I love. It's just long enough of a train ride, so that I can get a few chapters read of a book, but not too long of a ride that I fall asleep and end up lost somewhere in Harlem.

I unlock my deadbolt and literally run straight down the hall to my bedroom and shut the door. Before I started mopping earlier, I laid out two outfits across my bed for today. A modest but casual T-shirt dress and a pair of jeans with a V-neck long-sleeved tee. Now that I'm looking at them for the hundredth time today, it seems pretty ridiculous to wear a dress to watch football in my own house no matter how casual the dress looks. So I go with the jeans and tee.

I hear the door slam.

"It's me, Sabrina." Jason calls out. "Hey what's that smell? It smells fantastic in here."

"Some chicken I have in the oven. I'll be out in a minute. The flat screen is in the first room to your left."

I swiftly put on my clothes, try smoothing my frizzy ponytail, and waltz out to my first "working" football Sunday with Jason.

"Hi there."

"Well hello to you." He takes a longer look at me than I think he ever has. "I think this is the first time I've ever seen you in a pair of jeans."

I think it's his version of a polite compliment, but funny how the only thing I can think of is how Saint seems to like me in my skirts.

"Is the chicken ready?"

Oh, right the chicken.

"Yeah, it smells ready. Did you want something to drink while I'm in there?"

"Do you have any beer?"

"Sure do. I'll be right back."

As I walk towards the kitchen, I turn back around to take a quick look at Jason. It's weird having

him in my house. I mean I've always d
spending a lazy Sunday afternoon with h
never thought it would be because of a ⎯all
tutoring session. I also thought I'd feel more excited
about it. What's my problem? I decide to check in
with Marisol really quickly about it.

Me: I feel like I'm 14 again.

Marisol: Awww, why?

Me: Because I feel the need to check in with you about my love life.

Marisol: Love life?! I like the sound of that. Is my boy there?

Me: Don't be so excited. He's here, but I'm not on cloud nine like I thought I'd be. I don't know what I'm feeling.

Marisol: You're just nervous.

Me: Maybe

Marisol: He just got there. Give it some time. Stop overanalyzing everything, and for God's sake drink something alcoholic. It will loosen you up.

Me: Lol! I'll try.

After bringing out the wings, some blue cheese for dipping, a beer for him and ice water for me, I settle down on the couch making sure that I am sitting an appropriate distance from him. I don't want it to appear as if I'm under any delusions that this is a date. The word "professional" keeps ringing in my ears in Saint's accusatory voice.

"So right now these five guys are talking about all the games that will be played in the NFC conference today. Then if we click to another channel we'll see another team of analysts talking about the games coming up in the AFC. Each network has an exclusive deal with the conference games they show. The Nighthawks are in the NFC, so that's why we're watching this channel."

"Gotcha."

I should probably be taking notes, but how hard can this be? It's not rocket science.

Jason takes a bite of one of my wings and seems pleased with what he tastes. It's actually a family recipe. I have a lot of family from Buffalo, New York where any self respecting citizen knows how to make a good Buffalo-styled hot wing.

"Wow, these are good. I'm going to have to add a mile to my run tomorrow, because I'm going to eat a lot of these today."

"Good. I couldn't find any healthy football snack recipes online. Not ones that sounded good anyway," I chuckle. "So I made these."

It's no secret in the office that Jason is one of the most health conscious employees we have, but I do know a few things about sports and one is that most men like junk when they watch football, and definitely not crudités.

"Aww that's all right. We can make this our cheat day. No big deal."

I already had my protein shake and a handful of raw almonds before he got here. Hot wings would throw me completely off track. I only made them because I've been told that I make really good ones. I'm sure he won't notice that I'm not eating them.

"Look," Jason points to the screen. "They're talking about your new client."

"So do you think it's a slow start or is there something very wrong with Nighthawk's star Saint Stevenson?"

"Well I don't think we can blame him for everything that's wrong with the Nighthawks, Bill."

"Not everything but a lot. When there's no strong leadership, there's no strength, and Stevenson is definitely not leading the Nighthawks in the right direction this season."

"Or last season." Another commentator adds.

"I don't know where the Gunslinger is that we

saw back in Capital City. He hasn't been able to consistently get any deep passes into the end zone this season."

"His QBR rating is pretty low so far."

"I have some hope for the kid. I still think he can turn this around. He was the number one draft pick for a reason."

"Well hopefully for New York, Coach Ryan can do something to get that offense going today, or they're going to have another long and miserable season."

"Sheesh! They sure didn't have many nice things to say about him did they? I thought he was some sort of big deal in the league."

"He is a big deal, and that's why they devoted ten minutes to talking about him. Always remember that any press is good press for an athlete. Regardless of what they're saying, at least they're talking about him."

"I get the whole any press is good press thing, but I guess what I'm not understanding is why he's being talked about at all if he's been playing so badly for so long."

"There was a lot of hype surrounding him when he was in college. He was the number one college player both his junior and senior year. He won the Heisman Trophy which is the highest award a college player can receive."

I remember reading about that in my file.

"He also won Capital City a championship that same year. First time in the school's history. Plus he's from a football family. His brother plays in the league. His uncle and dad both played. I think a cousin did too. Not to mention that he's physically the biggest quarterback playing the game right now, and it takes several men to bring him down, which is called a sack by the way. The play in which a defensive player brings a quarterback down.

"Anyway it's really quite unusual for the quarterback to be so big that he's hard to sack, but in addition to that, Stevenson's biggest claim to fame is that he can deliver the ball deep and downfield with speed and precision. That's why they call him the Gunslinger. His arm is like a very accurate cannon.

"I just think that all the analysts out there aren't totally convinced if he's actually the real deal or a college fluke. He has yet to deliver on his number one draft ranking. This is his fourth season with them, and they're still playing really badly."

"I read up a little on our home team the Nighthawks. I see that they have had a pretty dismal record for a long time, so isn't that why they were able to draft Saint in the first place? Because they suck? Don't the bad teams get the best players in the draft?"

Jason takes a sip of his beer, and looks up at me above the rim of the can. "I don't know why I keep underestimating you, Sabrina. Of course you did your homework."

"Of course," I grin.

"And you're right. Even though there's a lottery system in place, the worst teams typically get the best picks in the draft. The Nighthawks didn't have the number one pick, but they traded up for Stevenson. They needed a quarterback desperately, and he was the best pick that year. That's why he's in a tough situation. The organization gave away a lot to get him."

"I guess there's a lot of pressure on him to deliver then."

"Twenty-two million dollars worth of pressure. Not such a bad deal to me. I'd take it."

"True."

"So you never talked about your initial meeting with him. Obviously it went well since he went ahead and signed the contracts, but did he say why he chose Carson Financial? I was just wondering, because the Stevenson family is infamous for not signing contracts with outside business managers or agents. His father is very big on keeping control of every penny. Did he have a split with the family?"

"We didn't really talk much about why he signed with us. We were too busy debating hoagies versus sub sandwiches," I laugh.

There's no way that I'm going to tell Jason the real story about how Saint Stevenson swiped one of my business cards during a chance meeting and only agreed to sign with us as long as I was the account manager. I take no pride in that. I wonder what Peter is thinking. His imagination has to be running wild about why this sports superstar would specifically request me.

"We did agree that learning about football is one of his requirements if I handle his account."

"And so you are." Jason smiles.

"That's right. I am." I smile in return.

"Hey is that your phone ringing?"

I left my cell phone on top of the counter in the kitchen and can hear it vibrating loudly against the granite. It's Sunday, so it could only be my mom or possibly Marisol calling. But when I pick up my phone, I notice it's a text, and I'm floored by who it's from.

. . .

Saint Stevenson: What are you wearing?

Me: Really!?

Saint Stevenson: I want to know.

Me: Jeans

Saint Stevenson: Thanks for that boring visual. Saying a skirt would have been much better.

Me: Are you always like this?

Saint Stevenson: I'm usually better:)

Me: I hope you realize that you aren't holding up your end of our agreement.

Saint Stevenson: And are you holding up your end?

Me: Shouldn't you be getting ready to throw a ball pretty soon?

Saint Stevenson: So you are watching:)

Me: I said I would learn didn't I?

Saint Stevenson: I like that you can follow orders, Miss White. It will make things go a lot smoother later between us.

Oh good grief.

Me: I'm not following orders you lunatic. I'm watching a football game with a friend.

Saint Stevenson: What friend?

Me: I'm pretty sure you need to be warming up or something shouldn't you?

Saint Stevenson: Pay closer attention, Miss White. I don't play until later at four. There's plenty of time.

I just assumed when Jason mentioned that the Nighthawks were playing today that they were the team we would be watching together, but I was wrong. Evidently there's a one o'clock and a four o'clock game on Sundays, and Saint doesn't play until four. It doesn't matter much for our purposes though. A game is a game, and Jason's been taking a lot of pleasure in teaching me the rules of pro football.

While this isn't a date by any stretch of the imagination, I'm having a nice time. He's only looked at his phone during random commercials, and he helped me clean up the mess we made with the wings. All in all, I feel like this was progress in more ways than one. With Jason and with learning the game.

So why can't I seem to get off of my mind the fact that Saint was thinking about *me* of all people on game day.

"I'm going to head out now. I'll see you in the office tomorrow."

"Thanks for helping me clean up, Jason, and for the tutoring session."

"No problem. Make sure to watch the Nighthawks later, and pay attention to the commercials. Maybe you and I can come up with some sort of strategic endorsement plan for both of our players."

Jason was given player Douglas James to manage. A newly drafted basketball player for New York City. Sounds like he wants us working even further together. Marisol is going to pee in her panties when I tell her.

"Okay, sounds good," I say casually.

I watch as Jason crosses the street and then bends over and makes a complete circle around his car with his hands checking for scratches or dents. I'm not really surprised. He's already expressed his reservations about living in Brooklyn (he's a Jersey boy), and he definitely loves that car of his.

I chuckle to myself as I'm reminded of Saint's comment about Jason possibly overcompensating with his car. Eh, like he's one to talk. I'm sure someone like Saint has a ton of expensive toys he uses to overcompensate his shortcomings with. Although I'd be hard pressed to name what one of his shortcomings would be.

Oh that's right, his personality.

I pour myself a mug of herbal tea and sit back down in front of the television, but this time with my laptop, so that I can take notes and start outlining a strategic plan. I've been thinking back on my conversation with Abby and it sparks something inside of me. If I'm ever going to show that I'm ready to be promoted to the next level, I'm going to have to make my mark with this Cro-Magnon athlete, and the only way to do that is to make the egomaniac some more money.

So that's what I'm going to do.

CHAPTER TEN

SAINT

I'm pretty sure that this day couldn't get any shittier. Even though it was only by a narrow margin, we still lost the game by a field goal. On top of that I'm going to be fined, because I didn't feel like answering any questions at the press conference after the game. They were dumb ass questions as usual, and I was pissed that they were waiting to throw daggers at me about my lack of performance. So I walked out.

I can't believe that the league expects me to take that shit from those vultures week after week. I'm not a machine. I'm flesh and bones with fucking feelings believe it or not.

I've been warned before by management to stop avoiding the press. That's why most games I try to answer some questions and avoid some of the others, but today I couldn't do it. We should have won that game and everyone knows it.

Everyone blames me, because I'm the star. The draft pick that this city has been waiting eons for. Fans are chomping at the bit for me to deliver, and I wish I could, but not with this ragtag team of players I've got backing me.

I can't wait for free agency status. Then I can finally leave New York. It would be the best thing for everyone involved. They don't want me anymore, and I don't want to be here. It's as simple as that. And the icing on this shitstorm cake is that my family is here tonight, because I'm playing in my hometown of Philadelphia, one of the Nighthawks biggest division rivals.

I feel a familiar and powerful thump on my back.

"Tough loss today, Gunslinger."

Kimball is the most respected veteran on the team and captain of the Nighthawk's defense. He knows how much I wanted to win this one for my hometown. Even though they're the competition, I realize that I have plenty of people who follow my career and kids who look up to me here, and I feel like I've let them down.

"Yeah, it sucked ass."

"No doubt, young boy, but let me tell you something a player once told me when I was a rookie. Everyone doesn't make it to the pros. It's not your right to be here. It's a privilege. And the real measure of how much you honor that privilege is how you face adversity when it meets you week after week on the field."

"I'm trying my best, Kimball."

"No, you aren't. Not by a long shot. Your head isn't right. I caught some of your games when you were in D.C. You're used to being the star of a team. The best player on that team. The best player in your division no doubt. But it's not like that in the pros, man. Everyone was the star of their college teams in the pros. Everyone was that go to player. So now you have to set yourself apart from an entire league of elite players. And the only way you're going to accomplish that magical shit is to get the fifty-three men here invested in helping *you* win week after week. *That* would be trying your best."

"I would've thought that their paychecks would

be all the motivation they needed to become invested in winning. That and the fact that losing sucks."

"Then that's your first mistake, and one you've clearly been making your last three years here. Most football players aren't moved and shaken by dollars. Real warriors have to be motivated by something more. Something bigger than dollars and cents."

"Let's keep it real, old timer. This locker room doesn't give a shit about me or winning."

"It's your job to get them to care. About you. About the team. About winning. I can help you with defense, but it's up to you to get your offensive men on board."

I slam my locker shut in frustration. I'm not angry with Kimball, but it's just a frustrating situation.

"I feel just as fucked up as you, Gunslinger. I've been busting my ass in this league for thirteen years and am only holding out maybe one more season, because I want a championship. I want a Superbowl ring before I retire, Stevenson, and you're going to give it to me. You just have to step the fuck up."

Now I'm ready to curse Kimball out, but not because he's saying shit that I haven't already gone over in my head a thousand times, but because this is not the day or time I need to hear it. At this point he's kicking a man when he's down.

"We'll talk about it more later, chief," I answer dismissively.

Kimball shakes his head and then walks away towards the showers. He's been in the league for over thirteen seasons, and he's definitely to be respected, but I think that if he had said one more damn word, I was going to have to pummel him.

I take my family out for dinner at my mother's favorite steakhouse. She always gets a piece of prime rib and a crab cake and my dad and I always get the lamb chops. My father and I are alike in many ways, but in others, we're as wide apart as two people can be.

"You guys sucked, Uncle Saint!"

Little shit.

Not only are my parents here but so are my aunt, uncle and my brother's son Jake. My brother Michael and his family live in Pennsylvania, even though he plays for Seattle. They both decided that they'd rather raise their children on this side of the country near my parents. So his wife, Kennedy, occasionally flies to wherever he's playing to see him, especially because they are trying for kid number two. Their son Jake typically stays back with my parents when she's gone, because he has school.

My nephew is a good kid, but he's twelve, and twelve-year-old boys are pubescent, annoying and smelly. That's just a fact. And today is no different.

"How'd your dad do today?" I change the subject already knowing the outcome of my brother's game.

"They won," he replies proudly.

"They always win," I say.

"Yeah they do," he replies chuckling. "And you guys don't."

"Mike and those boys are going to the championship for sure," my father interjects. "There's no stopping them. They've got their division sewed up already."

My parents love me and they love my brother. There is no doubt about that. I know that parents repeatedly say that they don't have favorites when it comes to their children, but for some reason I think my father has a soft spot for Michael. He's much harder on me and always has been.

"Michael did have an awesome game today, but the season just started. I feel it in my gut that Saint is going to make things happen for his team this year too. It's such a toss up right now. No one team dominates in his conference," my mother says with a degree of confidence that I don't necessarily share.

My mother is just as much a football fanatic as the men in my family. She has always supported and encouraged mine and Michael's dreams to become professional football players. Yet unlike my dad and uncle, she always made sure that the two of us had as much of a healthy balance as she could create for us.

Making sure we went to all school dances, making sure we joined at least one other extracurricular club when we were in school (I did ski club), and making sure she carved out time for us to concentrate on our studies and some public service activities. Athletics has always been the number one priority for my father, but a well-rounded life is very important to my mother. If only they made more women like my mom.

"That's so true," my aunt adds while my uncle stands there quietly. His lack of a response speaks volumes. He's either disappointed in me or for me. I'm not really sure which, but it bugs me just the same.

"Stop filling the kid's head with fantasies. They still haven't surrounded him with good enough players yet. It's not going to happen this year. What he needs to be thinking about is what he's going to do with his free agency status next year. He needs to get out of New York."

"New York sucks!" Jake interjects.

"Jakie!" My mother scolds as if Jake is still five years old and doesn't know any better. What he really needs is a good smack upside his head.

"Ma, stop babying the brat."

Jake gives me the evil eye. I bend over and whisper something to him.

"You want to go snowboarding right?"

His eyes pop up and he rapidly nods yes.

"Then stop talking crap about my team. Got it?"

He nods again.

"Saint, what's all this your mother tells me about you meeting with a business management firm?"

I tell my mother everything, so there was no need to tell my father that I've met or worse actually signed on the dotted line with a business management firm. I knew she'd save me the trouble by telling him herself.

"Yeah, I took a meeting."

"You got a problem with the way I'm managing your money? Stevensons have never let outsiders handle our money."

"I'm a franchise quarterback with no endorsements, Dad."

"You've got Lucky Sports."

"Okay so let me rephrase that. Lucrative endorsements."

"Well that's an agent's job."

Funny how that works. His brother, my uncle is my agent.

"Exactly." I deadpan and look straight at my uncle.

"It's hard to get you the elite endorsements right now, Saint. I've explained that to you a million times," my uncle says defensively.

"I'm sorry son, but your uncle is right. You've got to win some more games before you get the kind of big deals you're looking for."

"If there's a chance that this management team can get me a good endorsement without a winning record being a requirement, then I want to try. It's worth signing to them for a simple twelve month commitment. If they don't get me anything good within that time then they probably won't be able to at all, and I'll leave."

"So are you telling me that you've signed already?" My father raises his voice.

"Ooh, Grandpop is going to kick your ass," Jake

says without even looking up from the video game that he's playing on his phone.

Somebody please get me the fuck out of here. I need a distraction, so that I don't act on the strong desire I have to dump an entire steak dinner on top of my nephew's head. That's why I pay the check, say my good-byes, and call my adorable new business manager.

CHAPTER ELEVEN

SAINT

"Hello?"

Her voice is so sexy.

"What are you wearing?"

"Again with that?"

"Please tell me it's one of those skirts that makes you look part librarian, part stripper, part Lois Lane, part video vixen."

"You have a serious mental problem."

"That's what the team psychologist told me when I was licking her—"

"Shut up right this minute."

I can't help but laugh out loud. I love getting under her skin. She is immune to my usual Stevenson charm, and I find it utterly intriguing and refreshing.

"And stop laughing like that. What do you want? The adults are working."

"Just checking in on my favorite financial manager."

"I'm your only financial manager."

"Did you watch the game?"

"Yep."

"Good girl. So did you learn anything?"

"I finally understand where the red zone is, and thanks to you, I know what interceptions and fumbles look like."

She's such a smartass.

"You should probably be a little nicer to your ticket out of loserville."

"I don't know where such a land exists."

"Is that right? Well I did my homework too, Miss White. Your client roster consists of reality show wannabes, and let's face it, I'm prime time. So yeah, I'm the one that's going to make you a star at Carson Financial and get you out of a cubicle and into a corner office."

She sighs heavily. No doubt tired of hearing the unfiltered truth.

"If you don't have any pressing business to discuss, I need to get back to my life, ball boy."

Why is she always trying to get rid of me?

"Do you talk to all of your clients this way?"

"Just the frustrating *one*."

"Well this call is about business. I think I'm going to buy a new car when I get back into town. Want to help me pick it out?"

That was so random. I don't need or want another car, but I'm not ready to hang up with her. I enjoy talking to her. Playing with her. Plus I'm waiting to see just how long it's going to take her to remember who I am. Is she going to force me to start dropping obvious hints?

"You already have a car."

"I want a nicer one."

"For what?"

"Because it's nicer."

"Are you ten years old?" she scoffs. "As your new business manager I would strongly advise against that sort of impulsive purchase. Cars depreciate right off the lot. It's not a sound investment. Leonardo DiCaprio drives a Prius. Just one."

"Does every purchase have to make complete

fiscal and ecological sense when I'm a millionaire? And what the hell do I care about what some soft, baby-faced actor drives."

This woman is so serious. Way too serious and way too rigid for her own good. I'm going to have to save her from herself.

"Eww, who calls themselves that?"

"Calls themselves what?"

"A millionaire."

"Is it obnoxious to say when it's the truth?"

"Totally obnoxious. Especially from someone like you. I'd expect this sort of behavior from someone who doesn't know any better, but didn't you grow up with money?"

"We did okay."

"Oh please. Let me ask you something, *Mr. Stevenson*—"

She says my name like it physically makes her ill. This conversation is definitely not headed in the right direction.

"Why did you hire Carson Financial? Why me? The complete truth. If that's even possible for you."

I'm not a hundred percent sure what I'm doing myself. I just know that there was something endearing about her when I met her three years ago. She was alone, drunk and gorgeous. Not to mention that she had zero clue who I was which was something I hadn't experienced in a while. Even back then a lot of people knew my face. So when she didn't, I liked it. I felt normal.

Then I see her again years later. Filled out in all the right places. Sexy as all hell. Funny even though she doesn't know it. And still no clue who I was. And I couldn't help myself. There's something about her that I'm totally drawn to. She's not like the cleat chasers that I'm used to fucking or the models that I use as arm candy. Filling a void in her life with my success is not her end game. She has her own life. Her own goals and dreams. And she could care less that I could help her get there faster. She wants to forge her own path. Who wouldn't be attracted to that all wrapped up in a mouth watering, curvy, package?

I can't say that I know exactly what I'm doing with this woman. This is totally out of character for me. Ever since Adrianna, all I've had are a variety of expendable women in and out of my life. Nothing serious. Nothing even past seven days. But Sabrina isn't that. And until I'm sure what's happening here, I decide to stretch the truth a bit and tell her what I think she needs to hear in order to continue working for me.

"I won't be a football player forever, and I don't want to be one of those broke players begging for work from the league in fifteen years. You asked me what I want from you. Well what I need is some additional income coming in. I need endorsements."

"I could live forever on the interest alone of twenty-two million dollars."

"Well I'm sure that you and I live very different lifestyles. Mine requires a certain amount of funding since I like to go out and live a little. I don't just work, work, work like some people I know."

"Some of us have to work harder than others to make a living," her voice rises. "Some of us will always have to work harder than others to get ahead in life. In my opinion, what you really need is someone to help you make smarter decisions about the money you already have coming in."

"Pretty sure that's the same thing that I just said."

"Not the same thing."

"Did you ever tell me what you were wearing?"

"Oh my God, you promised."

"Wait–what did I promise again?"

"That you would behave and act like an adult if I allowed you to basically strong arm me into working for you."

"I am on my best behavior, Miss White. Especially when I've been at war on the field all day with a bunch of men who want nothing else but to kill me. Especially when what I really want to do is fly to New York and lay my head in between somewhere soft, warm, wet and very much female."

No quick retort to that comment.

Good.

I'm hoping she's visualizing the scene I just set for her. Me laying my head right at the juncture where the inside of her thigh and hip meet. My mouth salivating at what's awaiting me there.

When it's soft and beautiful, and I already know that Sabrina's is, there's nothing more satisfying then eating a woman to climax. I have to stroke myself a couple times just imagining it. I find myself doing that a lot lately since I've hired Sabrina.

"You're exhausting," was her only comeback.

I grin to myself.

I'm making progress.

She's definitely warming up to me.

CHAPTER TWELVE

SABRINA

A few changes have occurred in the office over the last few days. One of them being that without my input or consent, my cubicle was moved to a space closer to Jason and Samuel's offices. My guess is that Peter did it in an effort to give us more of a team feel since the three of us are essentially the new sports division of Carson Financial.

But I don't like it.

First of all, to the naked eye it looks like Jason and Samuel run the new sports division, and I'm just their executive assistant. That's because they are in two cushy offices, and I'm still sitting at a cubicle. To be fair they were already in those offices, but if we're a sports division team, with clients split evenly, shouldn't I have my own office too?

Secondly, the corner cubicle they've placed me in is by the far window of our floor. A very sunny window which causes an enormous amount of glare on my computer screen and makes my neck hot. The women who have small tropical plants on their desks like it over here, but not me.

Thirdly, I don't really need to have Jason a stone's throw away from my desk. He can see and hear damn near everything without any sort of fair warning. Like my embarrassing phone conversations with my mother. Seeing what I eat for lunch everyday. Or how about the moments when I simply need to adjust the panties out of the crack of my butt without an audience (which happens far more than you would think). I've got a wide ass.

Finally, I can't keep an eye on my nemesis a.k.a. Abby this far away from where she sits, and that's someone who needs to be watched at all times. If I'm not careful she'll sink her hooks into Spin, and I'll be stuck forever with an arrogant albeit wildly handsome football player. Speaking of the devil, I've got about twenty minutes to haul myself across town and meet his hotness at the car dealership.

Saint gives me a complete once over, and then checks his Apple watch as I arrive to the dealership on foot and out of breath. I took the train over and then speed-walked here as fast as I could.

"Five more minutes and you would have been late, Miss White."

There's something about the way Saint looks at me. The way he says my name. The way he licks the corner of his mouth when he watches me walk towards him or away from him. The way he watches my lips move when I talk. Especially when he frustrates me. Almost as if he likes it.

Almost as if it's foreplay.

Good thing I don't carry around any nonsensical ideas of having his babies like most of the groupies I've ever met do. I'm sure sports groupies are just like every other groupie I've ever met. Their sole mission in life is to meet, have sex, and procreate with whatever celebrity idiot they can find. And they find plenty. It amazes me just how irresponsible a lot of these wealthy men are.

"If you're going to force me to call you Saint, then I think I can tolerate you calling me by my first name."

"Nah, I think I'm going to stick with Miss White. It fits you. Respectful, prim, proper, and it fulfills all of my naughty teacher fantasies."

"I'm not your teacher, psycho. We're the same age."

"Can't your uptight ass take a compliment?"

"Funny how that didn't even sound remotely like a compliment."

"Oh, but it certainly is, and I'm being completely professional like you requested."

"I guess in a way you are behaving. I'm sure you're used to saying whatever to your disrespectful, slutty, anything goes type of women."

"That's harsh of you to say, Miss White. I don't slut shame," he chuckles.

"I bet you don't." I respond as a text comes through my phone.

And this is yet another thing that's changed over the last few days. Jason keeping tabs on me at work via text, and I'm not exactly sure of what to make of it. I know he's my mentor, but he's not my boss, and he's been insinuating himself into my business lately as if he is.

Jason: Hey, where are you?

Me: With a client.

Jason: What client?

Me: Saint Stevenson

Jason: Was there a meeting booked on the schedule with him?

In our office we use a shared online calendar that keeps everyone aware of what client meetings we have. We do this to keep things transparent, and so that management can see that we're checking in periodically on our clients.

Me: No, we just have a last minute appointment with a car dealer. Not really worth putting on the calendar.

Jason: Oh ok. The kid wants a new toy, huh? Lol.

While I know their first meeting wasn't the best, there's something about Jason's condescending comment that rubs me the wrong way. I guess I'm a little overprotective of my clients regardless of who they are. I feel like I can talk about Saint in a disparaging way all day if I want, but I'd rather nobody else did. I'm funny like that.

Me: No, he's buying something practical. I'll tell you about it later.

Jason: Look forward to it.

I stare at my cell phone going over that conversation in my mind repeatedly until my trance is broken with a question.

"I suppose that was your *not interested* co-worker again?" Saint asks.

"You don't know how wrong you are about that. He's *so* not interested in me, and yes that was him."

"You've known him for a long time right?"

"Yes, a couple of years. Why?"

"And this is the first time he's taken a serious interest in your work, right?"

"Yes, but I also didn't have you as a client."

"Exactly my point. Did you tell him you were with me?"

"Yes I told him."

"Ha! I bet he's in his office with the door shut, pacing back and forth, totally fuming. Wanting to kick me in the nuts."

"You seem to like to bet on a lot of things. You were trying to make a hundred dollar bet with me over Jason when we first met. Do you have a gambling problem that I need to be aware of?"

"I try to only gamble on sure things nowadays." He grins.

"Nothing in life is a sure thing."

"Some things *definitely* are," his voice rumbles. "At least I hope so."

I'm going to choose to ignore the way his suggestive comment makes me feel in between my legs.

Wet.

"So tell me, which of these cars are you thinking about purchasing?" I ask while looking around the showroom a little confused. Most of my clients like to buy higher end cars like Mercedes or BMWs. This is a mid-priced dealership.

"Which one do you like?" he asks my opinion about two different pick up trucks.

"Neither of them. If I had a car, I'd be more inclined to purchase a more environmentally friendly one. Not either of these gas guzzlers."

"I appreciate how you care about global warming, but can I make a case for wanting something just for the sheer beauty of it. I think that's important too."

"Maybe."

"Do you like flowers? Art?"

"Sure."

"Those are all things to admire and enjoy for their beauty, right?"

"Yes, but a bouquet of wild flowers isn't going to cost me a year's salary."

"If you don't make more than what one of these trucks costs, then you may be in the wrong line of work."

"You're so clueless."

"I get it. I get it. What you're saying is that you can appreciate something for its beauty but within reason. There are limits."

He has a way of making me sound so ridiculously boring.

"Let me go find us a sales representative to help us. I'm surprised they haven't met us at the door seeing that you are one of the most recognizable faces in this city." As well as the fact that I called ahead of time.

"New York is different than the rest of the country. Everyone here tries to pretend that they aren't starstruck, so they pretty much leave me alone. It's everywhere else in the country where I'm stuck signing autographs for hours."

"So that's why people at the restaurant didn't approach you but gawked from afar?"

"Exactly and it's kind of why I like it here. I can be anonymous and live a normal life."

"Of course that doesn't explain why you were

wearing sunglasses in a restaurant after the sun freakin' set."

Before Saint can retort, a man in blue slacks and a red and blue striped tie briskly approaches us with his hand outstretched for a hand shake.

"I'm so sorry for the wait, Mr. Stevenson. My name is David, and I'm one of the sales associates here. Let me say that our whole team was elated when we received a call from your office letting us know that you would be stopping by."

"My office?" Saint questions.

"That would be me." *Nimwit.*

"Oh I'm sorry, are you Miss White?"

"That's me. Thank you for setting aside some time for Mr. Stevenson today. We're interested in taking a look at a few of your trucks and seeing what the best deal is you can offer. We don't require financing, so we're looking for the best cash deal you can offer."

"We will give Mr. Stevenson the best deal humanly possible. He is a hero around these parts. We certainly want his business."

A hero? Give me a break. It's just a game, people.

"All right then," Saint interrupts. "Let's go find me another beautiful depreciating bad investment."

Poor David looks confused by Saint's choice of words, while I shake my head in silent laughter.

This guy.

Saint ends up buying a dark gray, metallic pick up truck, and I must say I was impressed to hear it was so that he could start taking his nephew Jake skiing and snow boarding upstate. I'm pretty sure my new client has a soft spot for his family, which is great to see. It might be the only genuinely humble part of him.

"You have time for lunch?" he asks.

"I really should head back to the office. I've got quite a bit of work to do."

"I'm not sure how I feel about sharing you with those reality show housewives."

"I only represent one housewife, Saint. The other two are on singing competition shows."

"Well I don't see why you can't pass them on to someone else and only handle me. Can't you tell that I'm an attention seeking whore?"

I quickly check my calendar and the time. "All right Mr. Needy, I can spare about forty-five minutes."

"Sweet. I know just the place."

"Where?"

"I'm taking you for a little slice of heaven."

"Pie?"

"No and stop trying to guess. Your need to know every single detail before you do or go anywhere is not good for your mental health. Live a little."

"Whatever. Let's go. The clock is ticking."

I'm in a restaurant the size of a walk-in closet on a side street in Greenwich Village with the largest slice of Sicilian pizza in my mouth that I've ever had. If I'm not careful, my eyes are going to roll to the back of my head.

"Heaven right?" Saint asks with an "I told you so" look on his face.

I nod my head, because I can't talk. My cheeks are full of cheesy dough.

Finally I swallow.

"The crust is amazing. How did you find this place?"

"It's a neighborhood haunt. Strictly word of mouth. The owners have been here for thirty years.

Cute little Italian couple. The husband still mixes the dough himself every morning."

I wipe my mouth.

"I guess that's why it's so good."

"So you're not from New York?"

"No, I've lived here since my NYU days. I'm originally from Colorado Springs."

"That's a big move."

"I wanted something different. Ever since high school, I've loved numbers, and I thought that I'd be working on Wall Street, which is why I planned on a New York school but plans change."

"How so?"

"I had a hard time making friends when I first moved to New York. I started checking out some local bands as a way to get out and be social, since I wasn't much of a partier, and fell in love with the scene. Decided I wanted to be part of that world in some way. Since I can't sing or write songs, I figured I could manage their money. It's my way of being part of that world without having to actually be the talent."

"Who's your favorite band?"

"Spin."

"I've got a couple of their songs. They're cool."

"They're actually one of the groups we represent."

"Why don't you work with them since you're such a fan?"

"Spin is a super group. They make more money than you," I chuckle, "If your ego can believe it. Mr. Carson's wife used to be their money manager."

"And she isn't anymore?"

"No."

I'm not going to elaborate on why.

"Well you don't need them anyway. I'm the only client you need, because I require your full attention."

"You really need something else to do."

"Something or someone." He grins deliciously.

"Do you ever stop?"

"Not even if you beg me to."

CHAPTER THIRTEEN

SAINT

It's rare that I see my brother. We're typically in completely different cities during training camp, the season, and during off-season he lives home in Pennsylvania, and I stay in New York. But we're still close, and our busy schedules don't stop us from regular random phone check-ins. Especially when one of us has had a good game, and Michael just had a hell of one yesterday.

"Hey there, young fella."

I always like to remind Michael how he's very much the older brother and getting older every day.

"What's up, little Gunslinger."

"Saw you out there kicking ass yesterday."

"Yeah, we're definitely on all cylinders. Something is just clicking for us right now. Feels good."

"How much harder do you want to kick me in my balls, Mikey?"

He laughs heartily through the phone. A familiar childhood sound that reminds me of so many memories. Sometimes laughing with me and sometimes at me.

"You'll figure it out. You always have."

I hope so.

"So what's this I hear about you jumping ship?"

"What do you mean?"

"Dad's feelings are hurt I think."

Oh, the money management thing.

"It had nothing to do with him or Uncle Greg."

"Then what is it? Dad does a good job of managing our careers. What would make you sign on the dotted line with an outsider? A company that dad didn't even get the chance to vet for you. We've never even heard of them."

I don't say anything at first out of embarrassment. I didn't think it totally through when I decided that I had to learn more about Sabrina White on her own territory. I mean I do really want her to find me some endorsement dollars, but that's not the primary reason I went knocking on Carson Financial's door. Truth is that I wanted to see her again. Plain and simple. I didn't actually think about how this would affect my family at the time. How it would hurt my dad's feelings.

"I know what it looks like, but trust me when I say that this has nothing to do with my opinion of Dad's management skills. I know he works hard for us, but this is a decision I made for one year, and frankly it's my decision to make."

"Defensive prick. Now I know you've done something stupid. You'd never do something so reckless like this without talking it over with one of us, which means that this probably has something to do with a woman."

Sometimes having a brother who knows me so well is a blessing and a curse.

"Mind your fucking business."

"I knew it!"

"I'm warning you, Mikey. Have you forgotten that I'm taller and bigger than you, and have been since I turned fifteen?"

"As if any of that matters. I'll kick your ass today like I always have little brother. That will never change. And by the way, threatening to do bodily harm is always your defense mechanism when someone's called you on your shit. Just confess. Who is she?"

"There is no woman."

"Well good then, because women are distractions. I should know, I've got one."

"A good one."

"That's why she's a distraction. I always want to go home, or fly her wherever I am. You'll see one day. Just not right now. When you finally meet the right girl, you're going to want your baby growing inside of her all the damn time. That shit is biological."

"That's not in the cards for me. I meet *the right one* every other night and that caveman shit you're talking about ... I don't believe in it."

My brother laughs even louder.

"I bet the chances of you going caveman for a woman will happen before you win a fucking game though."

My mood immediately shifts.

"You're such an ass, Mike."

"Oh stop your whining. I know it's not your fault that you've been dealt a crappy hand in New York, but at least you got a good payday out of it. And next year you can move to a team where you've got a chance of getting a ring and an even bigger check. So cry me a river would you."

"You don't understand the pressure I'm under. I've got the citizens of one of the most global cities on the planet watching me. Judging me. Expecting me to pull a miracle out of my ass every single game."

"Fans are zealous everywhere. That's football. You know what you signed up for."

"You sound like Dad."

"You're deflecting. The issue on the table is why did you sign with Carson?"

"I want better endorsements."

"You've never cared about money before. Dad cares enough for the both of us. So you're telling me that you left the one person who would make sure to get you every dollar he can possibly find for you to go with people who don't give a shit about you?"

"Did I tell you that I bought a truck? Gonna load it with gear and take Jake up to the mountains. Just like we did when we were kids. Just like we promised we'd do with each other's kids."

"All right, Saint. I'll mind my own business, but I'm telling you, Dad isn't going to let this go. He thinks someone's gotten in your head, and he isn't going to stand for someone brain washing a Stevenson."

"He's got nerve. Dad might be the actual cult leader. The Stevenson family cult. You're born into it and you can never get out."

And that's when we both finally *share* our first laugh of the day.

It's been eight days since I've spoken to Sabrina, and I'm starting to think of some very creative excuses for getting her on the phone. It's not until my brother's words from the other day start ringing in my head like a concussion that I realize what today's excuse will be.

"Hello, beautiful."

"Hi, Saint."

"Miss me?"

"It's only been a week."

"So you've been counting."

"How can I help you today, Saint?"

"Have you made any headway on getting me any meetings?"

"Actually, I have."

"Who?"

"During the week you have off–"

"It's called the bye week."

"Right, the bye week. I'm taking you to three meetings. I don't want to elaborate until I've confirmed the date and times but it's one sports brand, one soft drink and one luxury brand."

"Fantastic. Just the news I wanted to hear."

"Glad to be of service."

"Ooh, don't tease me like that, Miss White, or I'll come and service you right in that cubicle of yours."

She chuckles at that comment, and now I feel like Superman.

"Listen, there's one other thing."

"What might that be?"

"My father wants to meet you," I blurt out.

"What?"

"He's been my financial and career counselor for my entire life, and he wants to meet the person who wooed me away from the bosom of my loving family's protection."

"You practically stalked me and forced me into servitude. Do you actually want me to tell him *that* story?"

"Funny how we interpret a situation so very differently, but I guess that's what makes us work."

"Are you insane? *We* don't work, I work for you."

"Exactly, and I need you to keep that mindset

when I finally get you into my bed. I want you to work really hard."

"I can't with you today. I'm hanging up."

"Wait."

"What?!"

"What are you wearing?"

Click.

CHAPTER FOURTEEN

SABRINA

I'd be lying if I said that I wasn't a little nervous about meeting Saint's father. I guess for a lot of reasons. After some further research on his family, I realize now how it makes very little sense that Saint has signed with our fledgling sports division.

His father has a pristine reputation in the sports management world. In fact, it's so good that other professional athletes have inquired about having him represent them, although he doesn't do it often.

It appears as if the first generation of Stevenson brother's (Saints dad and uncle) bread and butter comes from their NFL pensions and their wildly successful summer combine that they run for student athletes.

They've been quoted in a few articles as saying that management is not something that they really want to get into full time, especially because it could be a conflict of interest with the combine if they did.

I feel like I better be on my A game in an effort to convince Saint's father that we have his best interests at heart. People that always want to keep things in-house have trust issues with "the establishment," and while I think we are a unique company with a lot to offer, Carson Financial is definitely establishment. There's no doubt about that, or at least that's the way it will probably look to Mr. Stevenson.

I regret how I've handled this meeting already.

I should have insisted that we meet on neutral ground. In New York. Being confined in a car for two hours with Saint in one of my shorter skirts is definitely not what I had in mind. He's already staring at my thighs.

"You ready?" he asks casually.

"To attend this very unorthodox meeting all the way in Pennsylvania? Not really."

"Think of it as a date then."

"Why would I do that? We aren't dating. Not to

mention that it's the middle of the day on a Tuesday, and this is a work meeting. A meeting which I put on the schedule, so will you take it seriously please?"

"Why would you put today on the schedule? I told you we were going to have a small chat with my father. Maybe some lunch. Not take a damn meeting with Nike. Honestly, you're the most serious woman I've ever met in my life. It's no wonder–"

"No wonder what?!"

"Nothing."

"Being *serious* is what got me my position in the company at my age."

"That's very important to you isn't it? Reaching a certain level of success within a certain time period."

"I have definite career goals that I want to achieve, but doesn't everyone? Isn't it important for you to get a championship ring sooner rather than later?"

"There are a multitude of outside pressures contributing to whether I meet the goals on my career timeline. Yours are self-imposed. There's a difference."

"Well if you mean that I don't have the pressure of twenty-two million dollars to succeed then you're right. You've got me there."

"I find it absolutely incredible that you are so

judgmental about the amount of money I make, yet your entire livelihood depends on the fact that I make it."

"Actually my livelihood depends on the income of musicians and television personalities."

"It depended on them. Past tense. Now it depends on mine as well."

"Not if I get a client like Spin. Then you'll be made somebody else's problem. I know just the person that would love to have you on her roster."

"You think that backyard band's money is better than mine?" he asks, as if I've totally offended him.

"I never said that."

"You didn't have to," his voice rises. "You've all but implied it by your words and actions since the day I signed on the dotted line. Would you feel better if I made my money writing songs about clean water and world peace? Is that what you like, or is the real issue here is that's all you know?"

"I'm sorry if I've made you upset, but I think that I've made it clear ad nauseam that I didn't want to work with you, and that I prefer musicians. So don't get all offended about it now."

"I'm not even sure what it is I see in you," he blusters.

"It's baffling to me too."

"Stop talking."

"Fine by me."

"Let's just listen to some music."

"Fine by me."

Saint gives me a cold hard stare and then turns on a sports talk radio station instead of music. I had to listen to it for almost ninety torturous minutes.

Sadist.

Driving almost two hours to Pennsylvania and meeting Saint's family over lunch is increasingly feeling like not a smart thing to do. But there's something about this guy. I let him get away with murder. None of my other clients could pull these antics. Of course none of my other clients look, smell or smile like Saint Stevenson.

I probably should have cancelled the meeting once I knew that it wasn't in New York. Especially since I can rely on Jason checking in with me like clockwork. This time with a phone call instead of a text. I'm starting to think that Peter is putting him up to these annoying check-ins. Now I'm going to be forced to tell him about this little day trip, which looks kind of unprofessional and suspicious.

"Hey, Sabrina. Just seeing how you're feeling about your meeting. Making sure you don't need a second man on the bench when you talk to Saint's father. I heard he's a tough old bird. What time will you be in the conference room, or are you meeting somewhere else?"

I can feel Saint staring at me using his peripheral vision while he continues to drive, so I decide to pour it on a little thick, since I was bamboozled into going all the way to Pennsylvania for this meeting. Might as well entertain myself.

"Dangit. I really had every intention of having you sit in on the meeting, but Mr. Stevenson didn't tell me until the last minute that we were meeting his father in Pennsylvania."

"What?! You're on your way to Philly right now?"

"Unfortunately."

Saint frowns.

"This is ridiculous, Sabrina." Jason fusses. "He's monopolizing your time. This guy is not your only client and taking a meeting with his father is not only unorthodox, but it was never part of the contractual agreement. You don't have to do this."

"You're right, this is ridiculous, but--"

Saint snatches my cell phone right out of my hand and puts it on speaker.

"Miss White doesn't need any mentoring today, boss man, but thanks for checking in."

"Mr. Stevenson, I need to say that it is highly unusual and frankly unnecessary for your new business manager to meet the old one. Especially when he lives a hundred miles away."

"What's your name again, boss man?"

Ugh, here he goes with that again.

"Will you quit it and give me my phone back, Saint!"

Believe it or not I am actually wrestling with a two hundred and forty-five pound quarterback, in a pick up truck, for my cell phone. Someone needs to be taping this. I could star in my own reality show.

"Oh right, it's Jase. Listen man, this whole mentoring mentee thing you two have going on is honorable, *not*, but you don't need to have such a tight rein on our girl here. She's proven herself to be fully capable of handling any situation that I may throw in her. Oops, I meant her in."

I'm mortified.

And I want to kill him.

"Hang up that phone," I say through clenched teeth.

"You heard that, Jase? We have to hang up now. You'll see her in the office tomorrow. We may not get home until late. Don't worry. My family's great."

Jason tries to say something, but I have no idea what, because Saint hangs up and hands me back the phone.

"Don't call him back," he orders. Almost as if he's ... jealous of Jason?

"If you pull one more juvenile stunt like that again, I'm going to ask that you be moved to another account manager, and I'll gladly tell anyone who cares to listen why. No one will blame me."

He says nothing in response. Instead he turns up the sports radio station, and we drive like that for another twenty minutes. Since I'm not used to him being so quiet with me, I try to busy myself by texting Marisol.

Me: I'm not trying to sabotage my career, but I'm not sure I can keep working with Saint Stevenson.

Marisol: Has it even been a month?

Me: He's a jackass

Marisol: You already knew that

Me: He's like a big kid

Marisol: According to you all players act like that. So why are you surprised?

Me: Maybe Abby will want him.

Marisol: You can't be serious. What aren't you telling me?

Me: Nothing

Marisol: Lies.

Me: He just gets under my skin

Marisol: Well put on your big girl panties, because if you drop the ball with America's quarterback, you can forget about that five year plan of yours.

I shove my phone violently back in my tote bag. I'm pissed. Saint notices, but still doesn't say a word. His silence is unnerving. I can't take it anymore, so I break first.

"Say something."

"About what."

"What's going on?"

"What do you mean, Freshman?"

"Freshman?"

I know I've heard that before, but I'm not sure where. Is that some sort of football reference? I observe him for a moment as we drive along the final stretch of the turnpike. I mean *really* watch him. He's grinning, because he thinks I'm checking him out, but that's not it. I want to figure him out. I want to understand why he's targeted me of all people. He's dated underwear models and famous actresses for God's sake. What does this football demigod want with me?

"We're here!"

CHAPTER FIFTEEN

SABRINA

His body is humming. He's excited to be home, and I can see why. Saint's family lives on what looks like a compound. About thirty minutes outside of Philadelphia, his family home is situated on top of a sprawling piece of grassy land with a huge formal stone house in the center and a smaller carriage house behind it.

According to Saint, it's not a working farm any longer, but it looks like one to me. I see a few horses grazing at the far end of the property and he already told me his mother has a lot of chickens. There's also a beautiful white wooden gate enclosing the entire property and a tasteful sign in front that reads Oak Hill Farm. For a girl from a modest home in Colorado, it's a real farm to me.

While I'm not surprised at the beauty of their home, due to the fact that the Stevensons are pretty well off, I can't help but take notice of just how good Saint had it growing up. How his sense of entitlement must have begun very early in his life, because he's always had all of this. No wonder he always expects to hear the word "yes."

"Why are you so quiet?"

"I'm not quiet. You are."

"Are you still mad about earlier? I was just playing with you and short dude. Maybe if he thinks he has a little competition he'll finally step up and claim you."

That's not exactly what it seemed like he was doing to me.

"Did you grow up here?" I ask ignoring that last statement.

"Yep and my brother still lives here with his wife, Kennedy, and their son, Jake in the carriage house. Do you like it?"

"Yeah, it's beautiful. You are very blessed."

"In many ways."

He says that while looking in between his legs.

"Why do you always talk like that?"

"Like what?"

"Like you are the most fantastic man in the universe. Like you are God's gift."

"You said it. Not me."

"You talk too much about yourself."

"I've got a lot to say."

He laughs heartily again, and it's so darn sexy and infectious, I forget for a moment how much he irritates me and laugh with him.

Tap. Tap. Tap.

We were laughing so hard; neither of us noticed Saint's parents approach the car.

"Oh hey, Mom. Dad."

Saint rolls down the window. It's not as cold here as it is in New York but it's still a cool afternoon.

"Hello to you too, Saint, and welcome to Oak Hill, Miss White," Saint's mother pleasantly says. His dad on the other hand just gives me a good once over and turns to walk back towards the main house.

"Hello, Mr. and Mrs. Stevenson," I offer brightly. "Nice to meet you both."

Saint's mother looks at me, then looks at Saint and smiles. It's a grin that completely matches her son's. It's warm and friendly and has a lot of meaning behind it.

"I hope you like lamb chops. I just charred some to death on the grill."

"You grilled lunch?"

"Oh we like to grill all year round here. As long as there's no snow on the ground. All you have to do is wear a jacket."

I nod my head as if I understand. I see that *crazy* might be a Stevenson family trait.

"Can I help you with anything, Mrs. Stevenson?"

"Oh no, dear. I wouldn't think of it. My husband made you come all the way out here to give you the once over, the least I can do is feed you."

"That's very gracious of you. Where did Mr. Stevenson go? I'm sure he has some questions for me."

"I'm not sure he does, now that he's seen you."

Oh he better ask me something.

I look at Saint with my best "what the fuck" expression.

"I'll go get him," he says.

Yeah, you do that.

"Oh that's cute," his mother says to me. "You two can speak to each other without words already."

Oh dear God.

. . .

The four of us sit down at a beautiful whitewashed, butcher-block, kitchen table to a lunch of very well-done but delicious grilled lamb chops, greek salad and couscous. It was damn good. Saint's mother is an awesome cook.

The conversation is pleasant. We talk about random things like shows we like on HBO, their plans to add solar panels to the house, and of course football. I was holding my own in the conversation until they took it there. They were mentioning things about players, games and coaches that I knew nothing about, and it was painfully obvious. My only course of diversion was to address the elephant in the room.

"So Mr. Stevenson, were there any questions you wanted to ask me about Saint's move over to Carson Financial?"

"Yeah, are you interested in my son romantically?"

I almost choke on the swallow of lemonade that is in my mouth.

"Not even a little bit, Mr. Stevenson."

That gets me my first smile out of the patriarch.

"That's all I need to know then."

That's it!?

"Did you think I was some sort of gold digger, Mr. Stevenson?" I ask a little miffed that he has no serious business questions for me.

"Anyone can be tempted by opportunity and everyone has their own agenda. That's why I like to keep things in-house. There's no questioning my motives, but you I don't know. I only want the best for my boy."

"I completely understand. Obviously I don't feel exactly the way that you do about your son, but I don't have any ulterior motives either. Saint signed with Carson, and Carson assigned him to me. End of story. His reasons for signing with Carson are his reasons."

"That's good enough for me then. How about we toast to my son and what's hopefully his final season with the Nighthawks. Do you drink?"

Somehow I feel like this is another test.

"Occasionally."

"Caroline, what can we drink with 7up cake?"

"Milk."

"Alcohol, sweetheart."

"Hell if I know, Clint. Maybe rum?"

"I think Miss White here likes tequila," Saint chimes in.

"Tequila? I don't drink that. Last time I had tequila was in–"

I snap my eyes up to his and the realization hits me. The sight of pure satisfaction spreading across his face explains everything running through my head right now.

"Georgetown." I finish my sentence.

"That's right, Freshman–Georgetown."

CHAPTER SIXTEEN

SAINT

"What are you doing?"

"What do you mean, Pop?"

"With that girl in there. What are you doing? What was that Georgetown comment all about? You've got about three minutes to explain before she comes back from the bathroom."

"It's something between me and her."

"Did you knock her up?"

"No, Dad."

"Did she go to college with you? Is she saying you two have a love child stashed away somewhere?"

"Dad, are you watching Lifetime movies again?"

"I can tell she's a nice girl," my mother interjects. Always the voice of calm and reason.

"She is."

"She's a looker too," she says.

"She is."

"You meet a lot of lookers though," my father adds.

"Not like this one."

"So you're interested in her?"

"I think so."

"I don't think she gives a rat's ass about you."

"She will."

"Did I make you this cocky?" my father asks incredulously.

"Yeah," my mother chuckles. "I think it's inherited."

"So you signed with Carson for a girl?" my father asks as if it's the most ridiculous thing I've ever done. Which it hardly ranks up there with some of the other shit I've pulled.

"That about sums it up."

"Then you're crazy, not stupid."

"I guess."

"Crazy I can live with."

"Thanks, Dad. I think."

"Shh, she's coming back," my mother whispers.

Sabrina walks quietly back into the room while staring at all three of us. I wonder how much of our conversation she heard. I can't read her expression at all.

"Can I talk to you for a minute, Saint?"

In the words of Scooby Doo ... rut roh.

"Sure, you want to see my old bedroom? We can talk there."

"Not even a little bit."

"Your loss," I say trying to lighten the mood. "I was going to show you all my high school trophies. Show you how badass I was."

"So it's like I figured. You peaked in high school."

My mother giggles at that joke.

"Very funny. How about I take you to meet Mork, Mindy, Laverne and Shirley then."

"Who?"

"The chickens."

My mother had the chicken coop rebuilt. This is the third rebuild, and I swear it looks like The White House. These chickens probably have a better life than some people. There's no way she's ever going to put one of them on the grill as nature intended. They're like her babies. Before I can point out each hen and my nephew's rooster to Sabrina, she cuts me off with a finger pointed to my face.

"So *you* are the stranger?"

"The stranger?" I play dumb.

"The stranger that I drunk talked to at the hotel in Georgetown three years ago. The stranger who must have been responsible for helping me into my room and tucking me into bed with two Advils and a cool compress."

The gig's finally up.

"Yeah, that was me."

"So why would you not tell me that this whole time?"

"I didn't know if that was an event that you wanted to be reminded of. You were pretty upset that night. And then once I realized you didn't recognize me, I didn't think I should mention it. So I decided to leave it alone. Up until today that is."

"You took my clothes off!"

"I sure did. You were sweaty and drunk."

"Oh my God."

"Oh my God is right. Have you ever tried

carrying and undressing a hundred and forty pounds of dead weight? It ain't easy."

"A hundred and thirty, smartass."

"If you say so, babe."

"And the Freshman remark the other day?"

"It was obviously your first time doing shots, and you were drunk as a fish, so I called you Freshman."

"How do you remember all of that?"

"It was a memorable night."

"We didn't–"

"No, nothing happened. I like my women alert and coherent. Plus I was supposed to get married that weekend. I don't do revenge sex. Not my style."

"And you recognized me in the restaurant the night I was with Jason?"

"Immediately," I say as I move closer to her. "And it pissed me off that I had to wait for him to make a mistake, before I could approach you that night."

"A mistake?"

"He took his eyes off of you."

I usually gravitate towards taller women like models and actresses because I'm so big; but I'm towering over all five feet four inches of Sabrina right now, yet I don't feel like I'm smothering her like I thought I might.

We fit.

"And I have to say," I continue talking as I walk her backwards towards the chicken coop. "That I'm a little hurt that you didn't recognize me at all. Ever. I must not have made a very good first impression. I should try again."

I'm making her nervous, but the kind of nerves that I like to see. Yellow light nerves. The kind that tell me that she's definitely attracted to me, but that I should proceed with caution.

"In my defense, I drank those shots back to back. I couldn't see straight."

"That's no excuse. I'm unforgettable."

"Saint, you've got me pressed up against a chicken coop."

"I've been waiting to do this for a long time, Freshman. I think the chickens will be okay."

Three years ago I was smack dab in the middle of a momentous year. I did what I promised my mother and finished school with a degree in physical therapy, I signed a record setting rookie contract with the NFL, and got engaged to my then girlfriend Adrianna. I was young, rich, and on top of the world, but I was also overwhelmed and had been for a long time.

Negotiating a deal when you're still in school is like walking a minefield. There are so many regulations in place that my father had to be careful of. So many offers to consider. So many hands to shake. On top of all of that I had to make sure that I was keeping my body in pristine condition and keeping my woman happy.

My face was well known in the sports world. They were always talking about me on television and when I did an appearance on The Kid's Choice Awards, that's when women my mother's age started to recognize me too. It was nice for a minute, but then it became difficult.

So when I met a woman, a beautiful woman, who was my age and had no idea who I was and didn't even really care, it was refreshing. It was nice to help someone out who didn't have any ulterior motives that night. She was just a girl who didn't know how to hold her liquor, and I was just a guy trying to help her.

I never forgot the innocent girl from the hotel bar, dressed like a corporate shark, but undressed was soft as butter and glimmered like sunshine. That's why when I saw her for the second time in the restaurant that night, I couldn't believe my eyes.

I had to touch her. To know she was real and not just an apparition. Fuck the guy she was sitting with. I had to know for sure. So I touched her briefly, barely touching the back of her neck with my fingertips, and that's when I felt it. That's when I knew for sure. My mind wasn't fucking with me. It was definitely the same girl.

"You're worrying again."

I can tell by the lines etched in her forehead.

"I'm trying not to."

"Put your arms up and around my neck."

"I can't reach all the way up there."

I take a moment to drink her in, because I know that I need to make a very important decision right now. She's way more of a serious person than me. She could get hurt. Should I stop this? Am I fucking with her head? I don't even know what the hell I'm doing myself.

She's standing motionless.

Watching and waiting for me to dictate where we take this. How far we take this. I have to make a decision. She needs me to make it. So I do.

Fuck it.

I bend down low to the ground in front of her and slowly lift up her skirt inch-by-inch keeping my face close to her pussy. I wish I could strip her bare. As memory serves she has a beautiful body worth worshiping, but there's plenty of time for that later. Especially because we're in my parent's backyard in the middle of the goddamn day.

I bend my head to the left and kiss the side of her hip, then hold my lips there for a few seconds. Savoring her scent.

"You smell fucking delicious."

She squeals with surprise when I lift her up like she weighs nothing, her skirt bunched up around her waist, holding her up by her hips.

"Wrap your legs around my waist and your arms around my neck."

"Saint–"

"Now look up at me."

She looks up, but I can tell that it's difficult for her to do. She's reserved, careful, conservative. She's fighting this, but even she can't deny what's brewing between us. What's been growing for weeks.

"Good girl, Sabrina. I'm going to kiss you now, because I've been wanting to for a long time, and frankly it's for your own good."

"God you're an–"

"Quiet."

I cut her off at the knees with a kiss. It starts off softly. Gently. I start exploring the inside of her mouth with soft strokes of my tongue, and she tries mirroring my moves with her tongue as well.

It feels sublime.

Learning how soft or hard she likes to be kissed. Familiarizing myself with her taste. And when she brushes her tongue across the scar on my lip, it makes my dick rise in deep appreciation. I use her hips to grind against my hard on, and I can't help it when a possessive moan rumbles deep inside of my chest from the friction.

I want her.

Badly.

But I only brought her here to pacify my father, not dry hump her by a chicken coop. She deserves better.

So I pull back.

"Saint."

Her breathing is labored and her eyes are closed as she takes a minute to calm down. When she opens them and directs her gaze on me, they're full of lust and confusion. I can see that in her mind she's running away from me already.

"Sabrina—"

"I think we should stop."

"Why?"

"For a lot of reasons."

"Were you thinking about them during that kiss?

Because if you were, I'm doing something very wrong."

"The kiss was nice."

"It was."

"But it can't happen again."

"But it will," I say confidently as I slowly lower her to the ground. Making sure that she feels every hard ridge of my body as I slide her down against me. Reminding her of what she's saying no to.

"We had an agreement."

"A gentleman's agreement," I say.

"Yes."

"But I'm no gentleman."

I bend back down and help her adjust her clothes. Smoothing down her skirt and inhaling her intoxicating scent while I'm down there.

"What are you afraid of, Sabrina?"

"I like Jason."

"Bullshit."

"I've liked him for years."

I stand back up.

"You're using him as a shield."

She's pissing me off. She's had a thing for this same man for three years. A guy who's never stepped up, and now all of a sudden that I'm in the picture he's sticking his chest out a little. Classic dickhead. I can't believe that I'm competing with the likes of this dumb ass.

"I'm not saying I'm not attracted to you, Saint, but we made an agreement and my job is everything to me. You're my client, and I'm interested in someone else. Let's not make things complicated."

"What the fuck is complicated—"

"Saint, are you out here?"

My father. He has the worst timing ever.

"Your mother's cake is ready, and you should bring Sabrina back inside anyway. It's cold as hell out here."

"Coming, Dad."

I slide my hand up the base of Sabrina's neck and grip the back of her hair. Tilting her head up to me.

"We'll talk about this complication later, Freshman."

And I give her another kiss.

"We've got a long car ride home."

CHAPTER SEVENTEEN

SABRINA

I've got a lot going on at work, and I'm kind of glad that I do, because it keeps my mind off of the fact that I've kissed Saint Stevenson twice and he hasn't called me for almost two weeks. I realize that he's been out of town playing two road games, but football is different than other sports. The team comes home to practice and then flies back out to their games, because they have at least a week between each one. So he's been in New York twice and hasn't called. But whatever. It's not like we're together or anything. And like I said, I'm busy.

The reality show housewife that I handle was just renewed for another season, but she's so broke that she's been calling me nonstop for a week to find out if her first check came in. This is not a good sign. Her spending is out of control. I feel a little bad for her though, because all she's really doing is trying to live up to the image created for her by the network. If viewers only knew how staged and scripted these shows were, they wouldn't waste their time watching.

I also have the opportunity to participate in a big meeting in about ten minutes that I'm over the moon about. Peter has finally convinced Spin to come into the office to discuss moving forward and invited most of the team to sit in. He wants our presence to show Spin that keeping them on board and happy is our number one priority.

Uh oh, here comes trouble.

"Hey, girl."

"Hey, Abby," I say flatly.

"Excited about Spin?"

"Sure."

"Guess I'll see you in there."

"Yep."

Abby heads towards the conference room then turns back around as if she actually just remembered to tell me something. Puh-lease. Whatever she is about to say was the whole point of her stopping to talk to me in the first place.

"By the way, did you know that Jason gave me one of his clients?"

"Oh yeah, when he was over my house the other day, he may have mentioned wanting to get rid of some new band that's been a headache for him."

Abby scrunches up her face as soon as I say *over my house*.

Ha!

"They're actually a really cool group. If this Spin thing works out, I may just get them signed on as one of the opening acts for their next tour."

"Sweet," I respond with faux enthusiasm and a saccharine smile.

"I actually need to catch up with Jason, before we head in the conference room. I'll see you in there."

She's looking for some sort of reaction from me, but I don't give her one. Not this time. And it's not because I'm working hard not to give her the satisfaction, but because I actually don't give a damn about any of it.

"See ya."

. . .

I'm sitting in awe of the three beautiful men in the conference room who make up the group Spin. The guitarist Ren. The drummer Paxon. And of course lead singer Marley. After a few minutes of introductions, coffee pouring, pastries and pleasantries, Marley doesn't waste much time getting down to business.

"So everyone, we agreed to this meeting because everyone at Carson has been such huge supporters of our career, and we felt that we at least owed you the courtesy of coming in; but having said that, the three of us have already agreed that since Priscilla is no longer with the company, we're ready to move into a different direction."

My stomach drops. Along with probably everyone else's in the room. We thought that the fact they were taking the time to come in was a good sign. Or at least a sign that they were open to being convinced to stay. Now it seems as if they're shutting us completely down, before we even get to make our case.

"We're sorry to hear you say that, guys. We've shared a long and committed relationship with Spin. One that we're very invested in keeping. Why don't you tell us some of your concerns. Give us a chance to address them."

"To be honest, Pete, we stayed with the company this long only because of our loyalty to Priscilla."

"Are you following her somewhere else?"

Word around the office is that Priscilla is starting her own firm, which would make sense. Her husband started the company with his connections and money, but it was her personality and attention to detail which kept clients happy.

"We gave it considerable thought, but we've grown so much as a group, and as men, that we feel at this juncture that we need to go with a company that is more aligned with our consciousness."

"In what way?"

"Well for instance, I'm sure your office is still burning fossil fuels. We are more interested in a company that is concerned with doing business in an environmentally green building. Using wind and solar energy. Composting food waste. Finding ways to reduce their carbon footprint."

There's an uncomfortable silence in the room. My guess is because there's nothing particularly green about a prewar office building in Midtown Manhattan, and there probably won't be for many years to come. It would cost a fortune to implement some of Marley's ideas.

"To be fair gentlemen," Marisol speaks up. "We

don't make decisions about office space and things of that nature. Mr. Carson owns this building, but he doesn't make building administration decisions. He contracts a management company for that."

"And that management company will do whatever the person paying them tells them to do. You're just proving my point—that Carson is a seventy-year-old millionaire who has no interest in what his impact on the environment is. On what world he's leaving for the next generation. We're not comfortable with that."

I think I'm starting to realize just how loyal Spin is to Priscilla. More than any of us realized. It sounds to me like they don't want to stay, because they now have a strong dislike for our owner. The philanderer. The out of touch CEO. And there's zilch we can do about that. So I might as well put my two cents in. This may be my only chance to speak to my favorite group of all time.

"Hi guys, my name is Sabrina. I'm an account manager here and can I just say that I totally understand everything that you're saying. I'm not going to lie, I doubt that Mr. Carson would be able to implement any of those suggestions you had in any sort of timely fashion. But what we could do as a team, is to make sure that we invest your dollars into investments that align with your ... consciousness."

Marley smiles at that comment, so I take that as approval to keep going. I start flipping through my tattered marble notebook and look for one of the ideas I jotted down for them eons ago.

"For example, what if we find a specific and local need in each city you tour in, and donate ten or twenty percent of the show's proceeds to that charity. What makes it unique is that instead of a general cause like say breast cancer, your donation would make a direct impact on the community you're performing in. Getting that community even more excited. Getting the press more excited about you, the concert, and the charity.

"And just to take it a step further, I took a look at some of your last tour dates. You had a great turn out in Hawaii, but did you know that Honolulu has a very high homeless rate in ratio to their population? A twenty percent donation to shelters in that city could dramatically impact the ability to serve more displaced families."

"That's a damn good idea," Marisol says. Backing me up like the friend she is.

"It definitely is," Peter agrees. "What do you think, fellas? Does this sound like something you'd like to hear more of? I'm sure if you give us the opportunity to brainstorm, our team here can come up with a lot of ideas that will work for you."

"Maybe," Marley responds then turns his body in my direction. "Do you listen to our music, Sabrina?" he asks.

"Yes." I smile. "You're my favorite band of all time. I listen to you all the time."

"What's your favorite song?"

"Treading Lightly," I say with no hesitation.

Marley smiles. "I didn't write that one."

"I know." I look at the drummer Paxon. "You wrote it right?"

"You're right." He smiles proudly. "Maybe I should write more."

"I've been saying that for years," Marley says.

"All right team Carson. Maybe we were a little hasty. We can give this thing a trial run. It won't hurt for us to stay on board for another three months, but I think the three of us agree that Sabrina here should be our point person. She seems to know us best. You cool with that?" Marley asks me directly. In front of the entire room.

"Umm–".

I'm stuck like chuck. This isn't my decision to make. I look to Peter.

"Absolutely," Peter says. "Sabrina is one of our best."

Abby looks like she's about puke.

"Yes," I chime in. "I would definitely love to work with you all."

"Good then." The band stands up to leave. "You'll be hearing from us soon, Sabrina. Even though we're in a transition, please make sure my mom gets her bills paid on time this month. She'll kill me if they're late."

"No problem. I'm on it," I say in what I hope is an assuring tone.

The three of them shake hands with everyone in the room and once we're sure that they're not within earshot any longer, the office erupts. Spin is our biggest client, and if they left us, it would have been a huge loss.

Woo Hoo!

Hallelujah!

"You did it, Sabrina. Spin is really yours. Congratulations." Marisol hugs me.

I'm still a bit numb.

"What in the ham sandwich just happened in there?" I ask her.

"You just saved the company's ass. That's what happened."

I receive several more pats on the back as well as one disgusted look from Abby, as she pulls Jason away for another one of her so called *mini meetings*.

"Can we speak in my office for a minute, Sabrina?" Peter asks.

"Sure."

Marisol hugs me again. "Smile. This is a good thing."

"I know. I'm happy. Just stunned."

I check my cell phone before I go into Peter's office. For some reason, I have the urge to tell Saint about Spin. Maybe to throw it in his face since I've been threatening him with them for the longest time, or maybe because I just want to talk to him. But there are no missed calls or texts from him, so I abandon that idea for the moment and go talk to Peter. I'm sure we have a lot to discuss, seeing that he's been temporarily handling Spin since Priscilla left the company.

"Have a seat, Sabrina."

"Thanks," I say nervously.

"You've been here for a little over three years, and you've made amazing strides. It's no secret that you've wanted to work with Spin in some capacity, and now I see why you do. You're passionate about their music as well as who they are as a group. You understand them."

"Thanks, Peter. I like to think that I do."

"Spin is a huge account. Trust me when I say that no matter how down to earth that they appear to be, that they are a lot of work. I worked with Priscilla closely on many projects and got a chance to see first hand all that's entailed with running their tours and their daily lives. They have large families, and they employ a lot of people. You'll be paying a lot of bills and putting out a lot of fires."

"Understood."

"I'm going to be honest and say that I wasn't going to give you or Abby Spin. I just didn't think either of you were ready to handle such a huge account, but I had to agree with the group in the meeting today, because they requested you specifically. And for obvious reasons. You were good in there. Like I said, you know them in a way that I don't."

"Thank you."

"But we have a problem."

Uh oh.

"What is it?"

"You take care of Saint."

You mean the jerk who I haven't spoken to in weeks?

"And you think I can't handle them both?"

"It would be tough ... not to mention that Saint requested that he be notified first if by some chance you were put on the Spin account."

"Notified?!"

"I didn't want to invade your privacy before, Sabrina, but I have to ask. Just what is your relationship with Saint Stevenson? He asked for you specifically when he agreed to sign with us. Or rather he made it clear that there was no deal if you weren't his manager. I don't usually agree to demands of that nature, but I was afraid we wouldn't get his business if I didn't, and we needed it. Especially if Spin decides to leave."

"Saint and I don't have a relationship other than a professional one. We had a very brief meeting in the past, but nothing to warrant him asking for me specifically."

I swear Peter is looking at me like he doesn't believe a word I'm saying; and as if it couldn't be worse timing, Kate knocks on the door.

"Sorry to interrupt guys, but Saint Stevenson is here to see you, Sabrina."

Great.

"Should I send him to the conference room? It's still a little trashed in there from the meeting."

"Thanks, Kate. Have him wait in reception. Sabrina will be right out."

"Ok!" Kate sounds happy that she gets to ogle Saint for a little longer. I'm sure he'll enjoy it as well.

"So I guess you're going to need an office," Peter says after Kate exits.

"Really?"

"You now have five clients. Two of them being multi-million dollar clients. That's a senior management load. If you're able to get Spin to commit after the three-month trial, you'll be promoted and you'll get your office. Think you can handle it?"

"I do." Or at least I want to try.

"Well your first challenge is going to be how you're going to convince your ball player that you can take care of him and a bunch of rock stars all at the same time. I get the feeling that he likes to be the center of attention. Especially yours."

"I'll handle it."

That arrogant ball boy doesn't have a choice.

CHAPTER EIGHTEEN

SABRINA

I giggle to myself. Saint is entirely too wide and long for the chairs in the waiting area, although he actually looks comfortable stretched out with his arms behind his back and his legs crossed at the ankles.

He also looks absolutely mouth watering. Freshly showered, dressed in a dark blue hoodie, jeans and sneakers, and I can smell his yummy ass from here. He makes it difficult to stay angry with him.

"Like what you see?"

"I'm not looking at much."

"Should we go somewhere private, so you can get a better look?"

I can't believe he's doing this in front of people I work with.

"Are you showing off for Kate right now?"

"Can I get you anything, Mr. Stevenson?" Kate grins. No doubt loving the exchange between us. More gossip for the office. I'm going to kill Saint.

He's different today.

He seems intense.

And he's delivering his one-liners with a little edge to his voice.

He responds to Kate's question without ever taking his eyes off of me. "Thank you, Kate. It's nice to see that someone has some manners around here, but I'm going to grab something when I take Miss White here to lunch."

"I already ate."

"You never eat."

"She's telling the truth, Mr. Stevenson. We had morning buns and coffee in the conference room not too long ago."

"Big meeting today?" Saint asks Kate while still basically eye fucking me.

"The biggest! Spin was here and Sabrina–"

"Thank you, Kate," I cut her short. "But I'm sure Mr. Stevenson doesn't want to hear all the boring details."

"Oh right. Sorry."

"Are you going to feed me or not?" Saint asks suddenly impatient. "Since you don't want to talk about your big meeting."

"You should have called first to check my availability. You've got thirty minutes tops."

"Well aren't you just a basket of roses and sunshine. What crawled up your ass today?"

"Nothing." Captain Obvious.

I take Saint to the first bistro I see near the office, and am waiting for him to complain about it. The more time I spend around him, the more I'm learning. Even though he eats a lot of it, he's quite particular when it comes to food. He pretty much sticks to a high protein and veggie diet (unless it's game day, then he carb loads), and he tends to pick high-end places a.k.a. places I can't afford to eat.

"I can't eat here," he gripes as he slaps the menu down loudly on the table. Boy that hissy fit didn't take long at all.

"Why?"

"These kiddie sized chairs are hard. I can barely fit in them." He wiggles his butt to demonstrate.

"The food is good."

I've actually never been here before a day in my life.

"All they serve are sandwiches. You know I only eat bread on game days."

"There's a perfectly good salad bar right over there."

"I'll pass on the serve yourself bowl of bacteria thank you very much."

"You're so high maintenance."

"No, I just have high standards."

"And I don't?" I cross my arms in front of me. "I'm not going anywhere else. I don't have time. I shouldn't even be here now."

"What's the rush?"

"I've got a new client," I brag.

"And who might that be?"

Isn't it obvious by the grin on my face?

"The best damn client in the world."

"You've already got the best."

"Better." I make sure to annunciate my T's.

"There's no one better." He pinches his lips together. "Who are you talking about, Freshman–*Spin?*"

"Bingo!" I mush his forehead with my pointer finger.

He laughs a little. "You're getting physical now?"

"I know how much you like that."

"You haven't even begun to learn just how much I like it."

"Whatever."

"So the meeting in the conference room today was for you?"

"Oh are you wondering why you didn't hear about it first?"

He stares at me with a guilty look on his face.

"I *said* are you wondering why Peter didn't call you and tell you first?"

"I guess he told you about that part of our agreement."

"He sure did, and I'm pretty sure that he thinks that I'm a kept woman or your love slave at this point. Thanks for that by the way. You're making me look *real* good at work."

"Snitch."

"Who's a snitch? Peter? He's *my* boss. He owes no allegiance to you."

"He shouldn't have told you, but no biggie. What I'd rather know, because I can see you're dying to tell me, is how you finally landed the big fish?"

"Well," I preen. "I dazzled them with one of my ideas for charitable giving by the group. They were very impressed. In fact Marley asked specifically for me to be their point person on the spot. Right in front of everyone in the room. There was no way Peter could say no."

Saint looks at me like he's bored.

"So Marley took a liking to you, huh?"

"Of course. I'm very likable."

"It's not good for you to have all of these unfulfilled crushes on grown men you'll never have. First Jacob—"

"Jason," I correct.

"Whoever and now this Marley dude. Do I have to drive a five year old Mercedes or wear clothes made out of hemp to get a little attention from you?"

I scoff at that. "You're just jealous that Marley makes more money than you."

"Think about that for a second. And you're supposed to be so great with numbers. Spin has to pay a full band. Tour organizers. Assistants. Not to mention all of their family members probably have their hands out. Me on the other hand? I don't have any one to pay except a lawyer and you guys, and my family is self-sufficient. They don't need my money. So if you think about it, I'm the way better catch. I can always take care of you in the lifestyle that you're accustomed to." He picks up the menu. "Such as it is."

"Good thing I don't care about things like that."

"Obviously. You seem to only care about your five-year-plan and your job, speaking of which, have you been watching my games?"

"Do you really want me to answer that?"

"What are you talking about?" He takes offense. "We won the game in New England. I was phenomenal."

"Brady wasn't playing. You didn't have much competition."

"So now you know all the quarterbacks in the league by name? Just yesterday you didn't know what a quarterback was."

"I'm a quick learner."

"I've got something you can learn all about right here."

He looks between his legs.

I change the subject pronto, because I refuse to let on that I've done nothing but fantasize about what's between his legs for fourteen days straight.

"And why do you always sit on the bench by yourself when the defense takes the field?"

He looks impressed by my high level observation.

"I'm going over plays with the coaches. You got a problem with that?"

"I think you should be talking to your players instead. Getting them revved up. Isn't that your job as the team leader? I'd think that you'd be good at that."

A waitress in a pink shirt and black pants finally comes over to take our order.

"Excuse me, but aren't you Saint Stevenson?"

Or maybe she could care less about our order.

"That's me, darlin'."

"I hope you don't mind, and I wouldn't normally bother someone like you, but my manager would love it if you would let us take a picture for our wall. We're big Nighthawks fans, and we love you here. You were amazing last Sunday in New England."

"Was I?" he asks while looking at me in that "I told you so" voice.

"Didn't you say you wanted to try and find another restaurant?" I say annoyed.

"Forget lunch. I always have time for fans. Especially when they are as sweet as you."

Oh good grief.

The waitress holds her hand up to her mouth and tries to cover the fan girl smile spreading across her face. These corny lines of his actually work, and he's delivering them right in front of me.

That's it.

I've had enough.

"I'll catch up with you later, lover boy."

I get up to leave in a huff.

"Wait." He grabs my arm.

"What?"

"You're crankier than usual. What's wrong?"

"Nothing."

"Don't tell me nothing. I haven't talked to you in weeks, and you're acting like a total bitch today. What's wrong?"

"Has it been weeks?"

Saint pauses for a minute then lets my arm go and smiles.

"I'm afraid to even ask this, but is it possible that you're angry that I haven't called you?"

"It's not possible."

"Oh, I think it's very probable." He grins. "You missed me. Admit it."

"Never."

"In between practice, eating and sleeping, I promised my nephew a snowboarding trip. So we drove upstate, and when I got back, I had to get right back to the grindstone. I'm sorry."

Phones don't work in the mountains?

Oh my God, what am I saying right now?

"No apologies necessary. It's none of my business what you do or who you talk to during your down time."

"I'm making it your business."

"I've got to go." I try walking away again.

He grabs me by the wrist smiling like he just won the lottery or something.

"Why are you smiling?" I ask irritated.

"Because you're so stinking pretty."

I squeeze my cheeks together with my hands and stick my tongue out.

He laughs out loud, and the entire restaurant glares at us.

"You look even prettier now."

I roll my eyes.

"You'd be mad if I kissed you right now wouldn't you?"

"I'd kill you," I threaten.

"Sabrina."

"What. Saint."

"When's my first meeting?"

"What are you talking about?"

"The meetings you set up for the bye week."

Oh, right.

"The first confirmed meeting is on Tuesday."

"Who's it with?"

"Wolf Athletics."

"Awesome, it's a date! I'll pick you up."

"It's not a date, and that makes no sense. I'm in Brooklyn, and you and Wolf are in the city. I'll come to you."

"Wolf is downtown on the East Side. Close to the bridge. I'll pick you up. What time?"

There's no point in arguing with his stubborn ass.

"The meeting is at ten."

"I'll be there at nine. Eight thirty if you're making omelets."

"Nine it is. I'll text you the address."

"No need. I already have it." He grins while patting the cell phone in his pocket. "Gotta go take a few pics now, and congrats on everything. I guess you're one step closer to meeting all of your five year goals, Freshman."

"Thanks," I say proudly.

His congratulations sounded sincere, so I guess I can put off questioning why the adorable creeper already has my home address, and why I'm smiling to myself that he does.

CHAPTER NINETEEN

SABRINA

It's like a scene out of a sitcom. Me and Ariana Grande are singing our little hearts out in the shower and the doorbell rings. I turn down Ariana just to be sure that it's the bell I heard when I hear it ring again.

"Ugh!"

It can't be him.

It's only eight freaking o'clock.

"Give me a second," I holler running to the door wrapped in a towel.

There's nothing but a huge mass of muscle in a

green military-styled jacket blocking the peephole of my door. I'd know those pectorals anywhere, and they belong to the one person I'm trying to avoid ever seeing me naked again.

"Morning!" He spreads his arms out as if I was really going to give him a hug hello.

"Why are you here all bright-eyed and bushy-tailed? We agreed to nine." I say waiting for him to walk in. I notice he has a bag of groceries in his hand. "And hurry up and close the door. It's freezing."

After shutting the door, Saint stands completely still and rakes his eyes completely up and down my body. I inadvertently start to shiver. Trying my best to ignore the fact that every time he looks at me, he makes me feel like the most beautiful woman that he's ever seen.

"Not a morning person?" he asks. His voice raspier than normal.

"Not really."

"I thought I'd make breakfast. A little protein to start the day, and then we'll go kick that meeting's ass."

I turn to head back to my bathroom. I'm dripping wet.

"Fix something for yourself. I'm going to finish what I started."

"Sabrina."

Saint says my name a lot, but he has never said my name like this.

Thick with want.

Heavy with need.

He's always playing around, teasing me, but right this second, I think he's deadly serious and if he is ... then I'm in big trouble.

"Take off your towel. I want to look at you. All of you."

I can't move. There's a war waging inside of me. My body wants to follow every one of his directives and I think I probably have for a long time now; but my mind is reminding me that he is a client, an over-indulged athlete, and a womanizer. He and I can be nothing more. Should be nothing more.

"Turn around *now*," he demands.

I reluctantly turn to face him.

"I just want to look at you. That's all. Open your towel for me, and remind me of what every mouth watering inch of you looks like."

Still not opening the towel.

"I've seen your body before, Sabrina. The image has been etched in my memory for three years. I just want a refresher and to take a look at how you've filled out in all the right places."

I take a deep breath and slowly untuck the towel from the top of my breasts and hold it open. My entire body is on display. It's not that I don't like my body; I do, and it's not that I think I'm unattractive. It just feels strange for a man to request to see it; that is until I look up and see the steely desire burning in Saint's eyes.

Now it feels extraordinarily sexy.

"Beautiful."

He drops the bag of groceries on the countertop and proceeds to take off his jacket. I watch with rapt attention as he deliberately takes it off slowly for my benefit. He smiles. I guess there's no hiding that I find him attractive.

After kicking off his shoes, he asks, "Now can you drop the towel completely on the floor for me, Sabrina?"

I take another deep breath of courage and do it. It's not that I'm a virgin or anything, but my sexual experiences have been limited to lots of lights off, missionary-styled relations. This exhibitionist stuff ... I'm not used to.

"Now turn around and face the table. Good girl. What a perfect ass you have, Sabrina. I can't wait to have it. Now turn back around for me."

My cheeks are burning.

This is way out of my comfort zone.

He walks towards me and holds his palm on the side of my face, using his thumb to brush gently back and forth across my cheek. He tilts my head up.

"Now I want you to relax. There's no rush. We've got at least an hour before we need to go. So take a few deep breaths for me, and hop on top of this table with your legs spread and your arms behind your back supporting you."

"Saint I–"

"Shh, I like to watch. Not to listen."

I close my mouth, slide my bare ass all the way on the table, and stare at my closed legs. Willing them to open, but they won't.

"Do I have permission to help you, Sabrina?"

"Umm–"

"I promised you I would just watch, but if I'm going to help you, I'm going to have to touch you a little."

"Okay," I hesitate.

"Do you trust me?"

"I think so."

He walks over, pushes one of the chairs out of the way, and settles on his knees in front of me. He places his strong hands on my thighs and slowly pulls them apart. Almost rolling his eyes towards the back of his head when he does.

"Fuck," he groans. "You're already soaking wet."

His hands stay on my thighs as he waits for me to lean back and support myself on the table. Once I do he lets go, stands up, and steps back.

"I've never seen anything or anyone more magnificent than you, Miss White."

I crack a small smile, because I believe him. I believe Saint when he tells that I'm the most beautiful thing he's ever seen.

"Do you masturbate, Sabrina?"

"Um, yes."

"With your hands or a vibrator?"

"A vibrator."

"I'd like for you to try with your hands today. I want to make you feel good, but I promised not to touch you. So you're going to have to do all the work today, okay?"

"Okay."

"I'm going to talk to you a little to help you get started."

I don't say anything else. My nerves starting to get the best of me.

"The key to bringing yourself to climax by your own hand is to imagine that it's my hand doing the work, because essentially it is. I'd start by stroking you softly back and forth across your clit. Lightly. Not a lot of pressure. Just enough so you know that I'm there. That's it. Keep a rhythm going."

I follow Saint's instructions, but I can't get out of my own head. I'm just going through the motions. I stop for a second in frustration. I want to be this carefree, sexual person with him. I can only imagine what types of women he's used to, but maybe that's half of the problem. I'm overthinking everything when it comes to him.

He notices me struggling.

"I'm going to come a little closer to you. Back where I was. On my knees in front of you. All right?"

"All right."

"Put your hand back on *my* pussy."

Oh my God.

"That's it. Back and forth over your clit, Sabrina."

He starts blowing softly between my legs.

"Good. Now move a little faster. That's it, baby. It's getting so juicy now, I can't wait to fucking taste *my* pussy."

His possessive words set my skin on fire. There's nothing more that I would like than Saint between my legs, eating me until I scream his name for the whole block to hear.

"I think you'd like that wouldn't you?"

My skin is hot and my breathing rapid.

I'm starting to feel a deep pressure winding inside of me.

The more he talks, the faster I move my fingers, the higher I go.

"You'd love it if I spread your cunt apart and licked you from front to back right on this fucking table wouldn't you?"

His filthy words have sent me to the precipice.

I just need one little push.

"Saint–" I beg.

"If you want me to give you what you need you're going to have use your words, Sabrina."

"What words!?" I pant in desperation.

"Ask me nicely. Say Saint can you please eat my pussy."

"Ughhh–" I groan. He's doing this on purpose.

"Ughhh?" He laughs mimicking me. "Those aren't the words that are going to get you to come all over my face. Now ask me correctly."

At this point all modesty has gone out the window. I'm sweating. My hips are bucking up to meet my hand. I'm basically finger fucking myself while Saint watches.

He starts kissing the insides of my thighs.

"Tell me what I need to hear."

"Can you please–" I exhale roughly.

"Yes?"

"Eat–"

"Keep going."

"My pussy."

Saint almost snarls as he pulls me forward to the edge of the table, spreads my legs wide, and starts devouring me.

I've never felt so out of control.

My hips are thrashing.

I hold onto his hair desperately.

And then I scream.

My whole body contracts.

And then releases.

Contracts again.

And then releases.

I almost think it must be someone else's pleas for mercy, because I don't even recognize my own voice.

Tears are welling in my eyes from the release of endorphins in my bloodstream, and I almost panic. I can't let him see me cry for God's sake. He'll think I'm a nut job.

"Sabrina." His bass heavy voice calls out to me.

I open my eyes and look down at this magnificent

beast, still on his knees, licking his glistening lips, and watching me closely.

"In front of me you can do anything. Say anything. Don't hide from me. Ever."

"I don't know why–"

"I know why. I know exactly why."

Saint stands up and pulls his long sleeved tee over his head while he watches me intensely.

"You need to understand while rules are in place for a reason, often there are going to be times when you have to break a few."

He unbuckles his leather belt and lets it clunk to the floor.

"I said I wasn't going to touch you. That all I was going to do was look at you. And watch. But I'm going to break that rule. I still want to watch, but this time it's going to be watching you bounce up and down on my dick until you come just like that again. That shit was fucking epic."

"Saint–"

"And that's another thing." His pants drop to the floor. "You talk too much."

Saint seems to take delight in the fact that my eyes widen when I see the enormous bulge bursting through his pair of black fitted boxers.

"I thought you knew why they call me the

Gunslinger." He taunts while he slides his boxers down to the floor.

"No," I say with a dry swallow.

"You thought it was actually about football?"

"Yes," I manage to eek out.

"No baby, it's because I'm packing a weapon down here, and I never miss my mark. I will fuck you long, and I will fuck you deep, and I guarantee to make you come *hard* every single time. Great thing about that is we both win the game."

I don't know how to explain this; things are moving fast between us in slow motion. Saint reaches around me, and sends everything that was on my dining table to the floor with a crash. He slides me over, lays his back on the center of the table, and then straddles me across his thighs.

I watch in obvious wonder at his cock.

It's thick and wide and looks as powerful as the rest of him. It's brick hard and is bobbing up and down almost angrily. My mouth waters just imagining what it must taste like.

"You like what you see?" he asks with his usual bravado.

"Yes."

"If you want it, you need to claim it. Mount up and take it."

I've had sex maybe twice in my life on top. Both times it was a dismal failure. One guy's penis kept slipping out. I'm sure it was my fault, something about the motion of my ocean, but I never cared enough to keep trying. So I certainly have no idea how to climb up on top of this weapon of mass destruction and make it feel good for either of us.

"Get out of your head, Sabrina."

"I can't."

I start motioning to get off of him and the table, but I'm trying to figure out the best way without breaking my neck.

"Wait—" He grabs my ass. "If you're not ready, then you can watch me. There's no way I can go to the Wolf meeting like this right?"

"I guess not," I say suspiciously.

Saint keeps his left hand on my ass and hip, and uses the right to start stroking his cock. Just watching him pleasure himself like this is turning me on all over again. I lean over and kiss the scar on his lip while whispering his name.

"Saint."

He strokes himself a little faster.

"Fuck, Sabrina. I love it when you say my name. Hell, when you say anything like that."

I sit back up and use my hands to trace the ink on the arms that's holding me still.

He likes that too and starts stroking himself even harder.

I grab his hand and lift it off my hip and slide my body down where I can watch him stroke himself even more closely.

He likes that as well.

Feeling more confident and bolder, I bend my head down and lower my mouth onto his cock. This I have some experience with. It takes me a second to get used to the girth of his penis, but I just start slowly and use my tongue to swirl and lick some of the pre-cum that was already leaking. It turns me on to give head, and I moan in appreciation of the taste.

He especially likes that.

I motion to replace his hard working hand with mine, and I continue the rhythm of his strokes without missing a beat.

His dick still enveloped in my mouth.

His hands now tightly gripping my hair.

Holding on as I bob my head up and down.

I get little warning when he blows.

"Goddamn it, Sabrina!"

He softens slightly in my mouth as I swallow

every drop, and then sit up with a wide grin on my face.

"Did you like that?" I ask already knowing that he loved every minute of it.

"Fuck Wolf Athletics," Saint growls.

"We can't do that," I argue.

"Quiet, Freshman. I rescheduled that meeting long before I even rang your doorbell."

This man's arrogance continues to shock me.

"So spread 'em. I'm going back in. We'll start with my fingers and then we'll work our way up to the big gun."

CHAPTER TWENTY

SAINT

The roar of the stadium seems louder today.

The stakes are higher.

We're in Texas.

The Nighthawk's longtime division rival.

Everyone is playing pretty badly in our entire conference so far, including us, but that's a good thing. That means that everything is still up for grabs including the division title and a playoff spot.

Sabrina doesn't think I listen to her, but I actually believe she's one of the smartest women that I know, and her questions about my leadership of the team made me pause.

Do I celebrate too much?

Was I disconnected from my teammates?

Do they struggle to see me as their leader?

So the last two games I've been in my teammates faces. Getting them laughing. Getting them angry. Getting them to feel *something*. Anything but complacency. Anything to start earning back their trust and motivate them to play for something bigger than their paychecks.

It's about twenty minutes before kick off, and I plan on turning things up even hotter for this game in particular for several reasons.

If we win it will send a message to the teams on the rest of our play schedule that we're focused, serious, and a legitimate threat. Second, this game represents a long standing rivalry that gets high television ratings every time we play, and I would hate for half of the nation to see us lose. And last and more importantly because Sabrina will be watching in person, and I want to be a winner in front of my girl.

I check in with the team assistant, Brad to find out her estimated time of arrival. I treated her and a few close friends to some seats in one of the box suites. She should have landed by now.

"Hey Brad, you did what I asked right?"

"Absolutely, Saint. The driver should have picked up her group, and they should be on their way to the stadium. They'll be in the East box suite. That was cool of you to invite the people she works with."

"People she works with?"

"At least I think they're her coworkers," he says reluctant to say any more.

I text Sabrina quickly before the Nighthawks are called onto the field.

Me: Are you here yet?

Freshman: In the van on the way there.

Me: Who did you bring?

Freshman: People from work.

That wasn't our agreement.

Me: Don't you have any other friends?

Freshman: Don't you have a game to get ready for?

Me: Who exactly did you bring, Sabrina.

Freshman: Marisol, Kate, Samuel and Jason. You happy?

Me: You've really got some balls.

Freshman: They make up the sports division. I had to invite them.

Me: No you didn't, but we'll talk about it later.

Freshman: Have a good game, Gunslinger:)

She's learning fast that it drives me crazy when she calls me that. It makes me hard and horny, because between she and I it has absolutely nothing to do with football.

Me: P.S. What are you wearing?

Today's game is probably going to go down as one of the most exciting of the season. It was a good old-fashioned shoot out between me and Anderson, the other team's veteran quarterback. First time he's been back on the field since a major back injury, and he looked twenty-one years old again if you ask me. I'm pretty sure he went to that back surgeon in Germany that everyone says is a miracle worker.

It was a three-point game up until the very last minute in the fourth quarter. Texans were up. I knew I needed to make something happen, but it was going to be hard, because the Texan defense had been blitzing me all fucking day.

We'd been running a play Coach B designed for the offense for an entire week at practice just for this very situation, but once I got to the line and saw how the defense was moving around, I decided to trust my gut and more importantly my teammates and change the play.

The new play would mean I'd have to specifically trust my tight end Cooper. A player that my brother of all people asked for me to give a chance a while back.

"Hey little brother."

"Hey, Mike."

"Thanks for taking Jake to the mountains, man. He couldn't stop talking about his awesome Uncle Saint."

"I knew the little stinker loved me."

"Listen I'm calling to put a bug in your ear."

"About what?"

"The man Cooper on your offense."

"New tight end? What about him?"

"He's the son of one of my old coaches at Georgia."

Mike and I went to different universities. Both of us on full athletic scholarships.

"So?"

"So I need you to look out for him. He's a good kid, and for some odd reason he's a fan of your arrogant ass. I'm not asking for much, just give him a chance."

"Mikey."

"Haven't I always looked out for you?"

"Yes but—"

"Don't you want to win your fucking division?"

"Obviously but—"

"So do your job. Trust your veterans and teach your rookies. Starting with Coop."

Remembering that conversation, I knew I had a split second to make a decision. So I decided to go with the play action pass. A play where I would get the ball, fake it to the running back, and then hand it over to my tight end, Cooper. The play would call for him to pretend to be blocking for me, then he'd suddenly break open, and I'd throw him the ball so that he could run it in for a touchdown. It's a call that can be practiced until you get the timing down a million times, but it's a play that really works best when there's chemistry between a quarterback and his tight end.

When I called the play, I could see the excitement and determination in Cooper's eyes. The Texans had been fucking with him a lot today. That's what's crazy about football. All the shit that's said on the field that the fans never hear. When analysts say that it's as close to war as you can come to, without actually being in a war, they are right.

Testosterone was flowing through our veins. Guys were talking about people's mothers. People's wives. Players were threatening to break each other in half. Anything to get into their opponents heads.

But I blocked all that out.

I had a game to win.

A girl to get to.

When I passed the ball to Cooper, it was a cathartic moment. A total release. Everything was happening without sound around me. All I could do was watch Coop.

Finding a hole in the defense.

Holding onto the ball like his life depended on it.

Running his fast rookie ass off.

And not stopping until he made it into the end zone.

The sound finally returned when I heard the

stunned silence of the crowd and the roar of my teammates and coaching staff on the sidelines. They were running towards me at record speed. Cheering wildly.

We'd won the game.

We'd won the fucking game.

And it wasn't because of me or in spite of me. It was a team effort. It was chemistry. It was trust. It was passion. It was a belief that we actually could do it. And while I know that may not be enough to carry us all the way to the big dance this year. It's enough to make me rethink free agency and staying with the New York Nighthawks.

Leadership, trust and chemistry are grown and cultivated. I can't just pick up and go to another team every time I hit a wall. No matter how good the players are on another team. It still would be like starting all over. And I realize that even though I've been with the Nighthawks for almost four years, I'm really just beginning.

"Saint over here! Amazing win today. Tell us how it feels to finally be getting your rhythm back."

"Oh I've always had my rhythm, we just all danced a little better together today."

My teammates laugh.

I've decided that I'm not going to do any more solo press conferences unless it's league required. That's why I've brought some of my teammates to the table with me. Today that's Cooper and Kimball.

Next.

"Saint, right here. What do you think you need to do to keep up this momentum?"

"Thanks for the question, Jim, but the answer still is the same as usual. Score and win."

Next.

"Saint—"

Brad walks over and whispers in my ear. I've got to wrap this whole thing up. My girl is waiting.

"Last question," I announce.

"Saint, word has it that you have you been strategizing where you might want to land next year since you'll be a free agent. Care to divulge where you might take your *talents* to next year?"

Debbie downer, Myra Kitch, strikes again. We play an amazing game, pull out a win, and she always has to put a damper on things with her negativity. Never mind that she says the word talents as if it's synonymous with herpes.

"All I'm thinking about is next week's game in D.C. Nothing more, Myra."

I get up to leave.

"Have an awesome day everyone, and direct the rest of your questions to my guys here." I place my hands on their shoulders. "The best players in the game today."

I'm starting to wonder if Myra's problem is that she's always had a thing for me. When I get up to leave she watches me as if the real story is wherever I'm going. Like she's dying to follow me. She packs up her things to leave too, so she obviously has no interest in asking Kimball or Cooper any questions, which is stupid. They were a big part of why we won today.

I'm already on a high because we beat Texas, in their own house, but that feeling only mushrooms once I see her pretty ass. I have to forcibly restrain myself when she approaches because standing right beside her are four of Carson Financial's finest, including that nutsack Jason. Gah! This royal pain in my butt has been sniffing up her ass so hard lately; it's taking every bit of self control I have not to say something. But I know I can't. I've promised Sabrina that we'd keep things private and professional at work. So why the fuck did she bring her coworkers to my game then?!

"Hello, everyone."

"Hey, Mr. Stevenson!" Kate waves.

Everyone says hello and congratulates me on the win. Sweet little Kate describes their flight in great detail and how lovely it was to fly first class.

"And we had mimosas for free," she says. "And a nice chicken sandwich."

"I'm glad you liked it, Kate."

I notice that both Sabrina and Jason are a little quiet, but I leave it alone for now.

"I thought you guys could get cleaned up at the hotel and then we can go to dinner and maybe to this karaoke bar next door," I say.

Something I had Brad arrange when I thought it was going to be some of Sabrina's college friends. I was going to win them over with good food then some of my bad singing.

"Can't wait," her friend Marisol says.

"Thanks, Saint." Is all Sabrina manages to say. It's bugging me how quiet she's being.

"You're welcome."

Jason looks silently between us with a sullen look. I wonder what that look is all about.

"You coming, Jase?" I blurt out.

"Wouldn't miss it," he counters.

CHAPTER TWENTY-ONE

SAINT

O*n the way to the hotel ...*

Jason: By the way, I met a friend of yours.

Saint: How'd you get my private number?

Jason: It's in the file at work.

Saint: What friend?

Jason: Her name is Adrianna

Saint: Why are you talking to her?

Jason: She's a friend of a friend.

Saint: Well she's no friend of mine.

Jason: That's not the story she's going to tell Sabrina.

Saint: I haven't seen that bitch in years.

Jason: She says differently. So Sabrina's off limits to you. You picked the wrong girl to play games with. Go find another.

Saint: You're about three years too late, asshole.

CHAPTER TWENTY-TWO

SABRINA

I've come to the distinct conclusion that people tell you not to shit where you eat for a good reason. Messing around with a client is bad business. I'm living this huge lie. I'm miserable. And now Jason is involved.

On the flight to Houston, Kate sat with Marisol, Samuel sat next to a business traveler, and Jason and I sat together. After the stewardess served us lunch and a drink, we started talking ...

"Are you a nervous flier?" he asked.
"No, do I seem nervous?"

"Yes, but I'm starting to think it might not be due to flying at all. You've been kind of distant with me lately."

"How so?"

"I mean I guess your busy right? Now that you have Spin."

"Totally busy. They have so much going on it's unbelievable. I had no idea it took so much to take care of three grown men."

"Yeah," Jason chuckled. *"I guess it was a good thing you got a little experience working with Saint under your belt."*

"Right! It's like three Saints plus all of these other people in their lives."

"So what are your thoughts about possibly leaving the sports division now that you have Spin full time."

I lifted my head off the window and turned it completely towards him.

"I didn't have any thoughts about leaving. Is there a problem?"

He sighed.

"A little one."

"What? I thought I've been holding my weight. I got Saint three major endorsement meetings, and all three sent over pretty decent proposals. I mean you

should know all of this seeing as how it's documented to death."

"Don't get snippy, Sabrina." He looked around to see if anyone was listening. "I'm just trying to have a conversation with you."

"Is this coming from both you and Sam?"

He sighed again as if our conversation was so painful for him.

"I know all about Saint Stevenson specifically requesting you be his account manager," he said in an almost accusatory tone.

"Peter told you that?"

"He's worried."

"Not worried enough to say no to Saint's demands."

"Why didn't you tell me something? I could have helped you."

"With what?"

"Sabrina, this is all a game to someone like Saint. I've worked with all sorts of players before, and while I wouldn't stereotype all of them this way, a lot of them can be real pieces of work. This guy's probably never heard the word no his entire life."

"I thought the same thing at first, but the more I get to know him, the more that I think I've misjudged him."

"What are you saying right now? He's the poster boy for it! That stunt with him taking you to his family's house. He was trying to convince you that he was a good guy. Meet the family. Trust him. I know it seems farfetched and ridiculous that he would go through all of this to get in your pants, but he's used to women who will do anything to get into his. He wants a challenge so badly, that he signed over a year of his life to Carson just to get it."

"You guys all right up there?" Marisol tapped the back of my seat.

"Yeah, we're good," I answered when I was anything but.

It's not like I hadn't thought about any of the things he was saying. I'd raised the same questions to myself over and over. I fought what I was feeling for so long and now that I've lowered my defenses, I wonder. Have I made a mistake?

"There's a reason why you asked me to go to this game, Sabrina. Just like there's a reason why your best friend back there doesn't know anything about what Saint has been up to. You know it's wrong and you want me to stop you."

"That's crazy," I angry whisper. "I invited you all here, because I thought the sports division would like to go to one of our client's games, and because Marisol *and Kate are my friends. There were no other hidden meanings behind the invitation."*

"You sure about that?"

"I'm sure."

After that I turned my head back towards the window and stared at the various cloud formations we were flying over. Playing every doubt Jason managed to dredge up over and over in my mind. After about ten minutes, he spoke again.

"I'm sorry. I'm just looking out for you."

"I know."

"I really like you, Sabrina. I have for a very long time. I didn't want to complicate our work relationship by starting anything serious, but I'm starting to see that may have been a mistake."

I turned my head back in disbelief.

"What?"

"You can't possibly think I would drive all the way to Brooklyn every Sunday just to teach you about football. I wanted to spend time with you outside of work, and I was using any excuse to do it."

"Why wouldn't you just ask me for a date?"

"I was being respectful of our work relationship. Like I said, I may have handled things wrong. But that's over now. I'm throwing my hat into the ring. I'm asking you to consider having a real and honest rela-

tionship with me. One where we grow our careers and our lives together in a true symbiotic way. One that you can tell your friends about. One that you can talk to your partner about work with. One that's going to last. One with me."

Saint didn't string together more than five sentences to me before dropping us off at the hotel. I've never seen him so annoyed. I'm starting to become paranoid. Wondering if by some magical way he knows all about Jason's confession to me. Of course he doesn't. But now that I've let Jason get into my head, I'm losing my grip on reality and questioning everything.

Gunslinger: Be downstairs at 7.
   Me: Okay
   Gunslinger: You're going to eat right?
   Me: Yes
   Gunslinger: What's with the one-word answers?
   Me: Just tired

Gunslinger: I'll see you in an hour.

Dinner is at a five star steak and seafood house. Everything is char-grilled over an open fire (not really sure how they do that), but it tastes really good and the room is beautiful. The restaurant has unique very long family styled tables that can seat up to five or six dinner parties depending on the size. The only thing I didn't care for was the moose head on the wall but I try my best to pretend as if it wasn't staring at me all night.

Jason stays close to me through dinner although we don't say much to each other. I didn't know what to really say after he threw down the gauntlet like that. It would have been nice to hear all of that a year ago, but now? Not so much.

Things have changed.

Saint is being his usual outgoing self. Flirting with waitresses. Ordering drinks. Graciously giving autographs to the line of people that seemed to recognize him. Yet through it all, I can feel him watching me carefully out of the corner of his eye.

When it's karaoke time, I'm ready to go back to my room and go to sleep. I don't feel like singing, but there was no way Marisol or bubbly Kate were ever going to go for that. They were in Texas, and they wanted to party.

Sam goes first. He's a quiet man. Married with two kids and he keeps to himself, but I could tell that this was a trip he couldn't wait to tell his buddies all about. He's oblivious to all of our drama and seems to genuinely enjoy the evening and Saint. His song selection is the old classic Hall & Oates song "Private Eyes." An appropriate selection for the evening.

Next up is Marisol. She's miffed that they don't have any current salsa hits by balladeer Marc Anthony to choose from, so she settles with "Rhythm is Gonna Get You" by Gloria Estefan. Marisol can actually carry a tune and is probably going to be the best singer of the night.

Kate steps up next and thankfully brings the room into the twenty-first century with "Ex's and Oh's" by Elle King. She drags me up kicking and screaming for the latter part of the song, but I'm glad that she does, because it raises my spirits and temporarily gets me out of my own thoughts.

Jason asks me to sing the "A Whole New World" duet from the Disney movie *Aladdin*, but when I decline, he decides to pass on performing a song altogether. Then sits there with a screwed up face.

Saint on the other hand is feeling no pain and it's

almost as if he's chomping at the bit to sing. I know this is going to be bad. I just didn't know how bad. His song selection is Ginuwine's "Pony." Complete with raunchy stripper moves and dedicated especially to me.

He's a little angry.

And a lot drunk.

I know the best thing would be to cut the night short and get him back to the hotel where he can sleep it off.

But after his last pony gyration in front of my face, and a lot of Marisol and Kate's whooping and hollering to add fuel to the fire, Jason can't take it anymore. So he stands up and yokes Saint back by the neck.

Then fists started flying.

Sam tries to get in between them and accidentally gets clocked in the eye.

Kate is screaming.

Marisol runs out the room to get some help.

And I am literally on Saint's back.

"Get off me!" he yells and swings.

I'm not sure if he is yelling at me, Jason, or both of us but I'm not budging. I hope that if I don't get off of him, he'll eventually stop. I can't even believe they are scuffling this long. That's how I know Saint's drunk. Sober he would have been able to put someone like Jason down with one swing.

"Stop it, Saint," I beg.

"Fuck that!" he roars. "I'm sick of this motherfucker."

Marisol comes running back in and speaks to the room like a high school principal.

"The police are going to be called in three minutes if you don't stop right now, Mr. Stevenson. Is that the kind of press you want after the game you've had today!?"

Saint stops moving, but is still holding Jason by the collar.

I'm still on Saint's back relieved that they've stopped.

Jason puts his hands down, but is glaring at me now.

"Have you already slept with him?" he asks incredulously. "You couldn't be that stupid."

And that's when Saint knocks Jason to the floor with one strong jab. Face first. Jason's mouth hits the tile floor and a tooth flies out and slides across the floor.

"Don't you ever fucking talk to her like that again."

I'm stunned.

Completely stunned at the mess I've created.

I slide down Saint's back and run out of the room.

Marisol follows me.

"What just happened in there?"

"I'm not totally sure."

"You know more than I do."

"I'm sleeping with Saint."

"Oh my God!"

"And Jason just told me on the plane that he has feelings for me."

"Double damn."

"And I think they're both angry at me at this point."

"You think?"

"I know what you're thinking, Marisol."

"No you don't, and it doesn't matter what I'm thinking. All that matters is that first my friend is all right and second that you'll have a job on Monday. I'll talk to Jason after I get him to an emergency dentist."

"I'm not sure it will work. I think Peter and Jason are in cahoots."

"Peter does whatever is in Carson Financial's best interest. You just might be more valuable nowadays than any of us."

"Really? Because I feel like a bad luck penny. I don't know what I'm doing, Marisol."

"Do what your heart tells you to do, and I promise you that things will always work out as they should."

God I hope that's true.

CHAPTER TWENTY-THREE

SAINT

"My fucking head."

I know a hangover when I feel one.

"I bet it hurts."

"Where am I?"

My voice sounds scratchy.

"In your luxurious hotel suite that I hope the league pays for."

I'm in my room, but I don't remember how I got here. I do remember getting into a fight with that tiny-tot Jason over the traitorous woman lying in my bed right now. I hope I put that slug in the hospital.

"Where is everyone?"

"They decided to fly out this morning."

"Everyone?"

"Yes, everyone."

Guess I didn't put his ass in the hospital.

"Why are *you* here?"

"What kind of question is that? Here take these."

Sabrina hands me a glass of water and two pills.

"I can't see what these are. It's dark in here. Are you trying to kill me?"

"The drapes are shut. It was inevitable that you were going to need to sleep in after the night you had. And all it is, is some water and some painkillers. The same thing you did for me three years ago in a hotel room in Georgetown."

"I didn't spend the night though."

"Well I'm slutty like that. So I stayed."

I want to laugh, but my head still hurts.

"I shouldn't be in this much pain. I had three drinks."

"Three times three."

"What was *that* last night?"

"What was what?"

"What the fuck is going on between you and Jackson?"

"Nothing is going on between me and *Jason*. I

thought something was going on between me and you."

"Don't try and sweet talk me now, Freshman."

"Why?"

She climbs on top of me. She's so damn beautiful.

"I'm not in the mood," I lie.

She looks down at my morning wood.

"Something tells me you're always in the mood, Gunslinger."

"That's just biology. Don't flatter yourself."

"What are we doing, Saint?"

"Well you're crushing my legs right now."

"I'll move up higher then."

She's trying to seduce me, but I'm still angry, probably most at myself.

"Don't sit on that. I have to pee."

"Ugh! Then go pee."

I go to the bathroom and look at myself. I look like death warmed over. I can't believe I let that little shrimp get into my head, but as I sober up, I'm starting to realize why.

I'm in love with Sabrina White.

I love her so much that I was scared shitless that he was about to snatch her away from me. I wouldn't put it past Adriana to tell whatever lies she wanted to, to fuck with me. Especially after she came crawling back to me a month after she left me at the altar, and I shut the door on her. Literally and figuratively. It's incredible how the guilty ones can hold a grudge the longest.

I splash some water on my face and take a piss. I know I've got some hands to shake and babies to kiss to make this go away for Sabrina. Her job means everything to her. I fucked up last night. I outed us and fought one of her coworkers all in one night. I'm surprised she's even speaking to me.

"Did you work your way through school as a stripper?" She asks through the bathroom door.

"I didn't have to work my way through school, Freshman."

"Oh that's right, you come from a chicken farm where the chickens get to live forever."

I open the door.

"You're real funny."

"Am I?"

"You're real pretty too."

"Am I?"

"The prettiest."

"I'll ask you again. What are we doing?"

"We're falling in love."

"We are?"

"I definitely am. Aren't you?"

I pray to God her answer is yes.

"And you're ready for one woman?" she asks.

She can't be serious.

"There's only been you since the minute I saw you again at the restaurant, Sabrina. I only see you."

"What about this text Jason sent me? What about your ex Adriana?"

"You know all there is to know. She was my college girlfriend who left me high and dry on our wedding day. But believe me when I say that her leaving me was nothing but the universe correcting its course and correcting my life. It had to happen, so that I would meet you."

"Are you sure you're over her? You sound angry when you talk about her."

"I was a kid, Sabrina, and of course I was angry. It was embarrassing as shit to be jilted like that. But there's nothing about not having her in my life that I regret. I only see you."

She swallows. "And I only see you."

I'm relieved to hear it.

"What did you think of my game?"

"I thought you did an amazing job leading your team to victory. You were awesome."

I beam with pride.

"Will you come to next week's game?"

"It's possible since I may have a lot of free time on my hands after this weekend."

"I'll fix it. I promise. Or you know what? You can leave Carson and start your own firm. Would you like that?"

"With you as my only client?" She smiles wrapping her arms around my waist.

"Me and Spin."

"Are you insane? Spin barely knows me. They're not following me anywhere."

"Who do you think convinced them to meet with Carson one more time?"

She steps back. "What are you talking about?"

"The world is a small place, babe. Marley's younger brother had been to a Stevenson Summer Combine several years ago. My family knows his family."

"Funny how you never mentioned that."

"We aren't best buds, but I may have told him his number one fan worked up there, and that I'd owe him one if he took a meeting."

"So he wasn't dazzled by me. It was all a set up," she says disappointed.

"Partially a set up."

I pull her to me again and lift her chin. I need her to know how sincere I am.

"I never told them what your name was, and we made no agreement that they'd have to stay on. The only deal we made was to give you guys a meeting. They were drawn to you specifically all on their own, and because of whatever you told them in there."

"And Peter?"

"All I asked him to do was give me a call if Spin called a meeting, and to make sure that you were sitting in on any meeting if they did. Little fucker didn't call me though, but at least you were there."

"Why'd you do all of this, Saint?"

"Because I was falling in love with you, and even though I didn't know it at the time, I knew that I wanted to help you reach your five-year goals. I wanted to be the man to help you get there. To make you happy. And now I want to be the man that helps you plan your next five years and your next fifty–if you let me."

She kisses me tenderly on the lips.

"Thank you."

"Why are you wearing all those clothes, and I'm just wearing these?"

I look down at my boxers.

"You know how exhausting it was peeling off the

clothes of a two hundred forty-five pound quarterback?" She giggles throwing my words back at me. "I didn't have the energy to take mine off too."

"Let me help you then." I trail my knuckles down the side of her face.

I raise Sabrina's arms and slowly peel off her blouse and bra, but I leave the skirt. I love her in it. I've jerked myself off to the images of her in them when I'm on the road. So it stays.

"It's been a while since you've been in my bed," I say to her.

"We've never done it in a bed."

"Damn, we haven't?"

"You're very impulsive."

"Well let me rephrase that by saying it's been a while since I've been inside of you."

"You're a very busy man."

"I'm never too busy to give my lady what she needs."

"And what do I need?"

"Me inside of you today, tomorrow, and the next day, and the day after that—"

She starts laughing and it's the most sublime thing I've ever heard.

"You'd have to take me everywhere to make that happen."

"I wish that were possible, Sabrina, because believe me I would."

She smiles and slides her fingertips down the side of my face.

"Well let's worry about today for now. You, me, in a bed. Make love to me, Saint."

"Your wish is my command. Get on the bed, baby."

Sabrina lies down, and I sit up on my knees between her legs. I lift her hips and keep them at a raised angle on my thighs. Her knees bent. Then I slide my hands under her skirt and pull her panties down and off.

"You don't need to ever wear these again," I say twirling them around my pointer finger before I fling them to the floor. "They just get in the way."

"Of course you'd say that—"

I silence her smart mouth quickly by sliding two of my fingers inside her slick pussy.

"What'd you say?" I tease while pumping them in and out of her. Making sure to simultaneously rub her clit with my thumb.

"Nothing now," she breathlessly answers.

"Exactly."

I pump harder and faster but keep a close eye on her breathing. I know when she's getting close to coming by how quickly her chest rises and falls. If I give myself another month, I'll be the master and commander of all of her orgasms.

"I need you inside me," she begs.

Like music to my years.

I slide her skirt up farther so that it bunches completely around her waist and look at her pussy. It's wet and beautiful and all mine. I lift it much higher and bend my head down to give it a kiss.

Then a lick.

Then I suck really hard on her clit and hold the suction for a few seconds.

I can hear her gripping the sheets tightly.

"Please–" she begs, and then I release her instantly.

I lower her back down and swiftly slide her farther forward, lining my cock up to the entrance of my favorite place to play.

"This is going to be deep and long," I promise her as I hold onto her waist and push myself deep inside of her.

Waiting a second for her to become adjusted to my size. At this angle I get really deep and it feels exquisite.

She bites her bottom lip. "I'm ready."

As I start getting deep inside of Sabrina's pussy, her moans start to turn to mewls, but I'm not ready for her to come yet, so I slide out, and turn her over on all fours. I playfully slap her ass once on each cheek, line myself back up, and enter her from behind.

"Even deeper," I groan.

She loves it and starts fucking me back.

Hard.

Her hair is conveniently in a ponytail, so I grab the end of it and pull her head back while I lick and kiss the side of her neck. Her groans are getting louder and my dick is swelling larger by the second as I stroke in and out.

"Whose pussy is this?" I demand to know.

"Yours."

"Whose!"

"Yours!"

She's almost there and there's no stopping that big orgasm train even if I wanted to. So I pull myself almost completely out of her, slap her ass one more time, then I ram all the way back home.

"Come for me."

Her orgasm hits her hard and fast. My name rolling off her lips like I am her alpha and omega. That shit makes me feel like a god. Her god.

The sound of her release sends me swiftly to mine.

"Fuck, baby. I love you," I groan.

"I love you too," she exhales.

Our bodies lay in a shuddering, sweaty mess.

We're both floating high on a cloud of post orgasm twilight.

I'm now on my back and have her pulled into my side. Her ponytail has since come apart, so I slide the wisps of hair out of her face. I kiss the top of her head, thanking whoever is out there watching over me for sending Sabrina to me.

"Would you do something for me, Saint?"

"Anything, baby."

She rolls over to the nightstand and picks up her phone. After a few swipes, she pulls up a song, presses play, and turns up the volume.

It's Ginuwine's "Pony."

Shit.

"Dance for me again," She demands mischievously.

"Go put your skirt back on and I will."

She smiles, slides on her skirt, and then hits play.

"Game on, Gunslinger."

CHAPTER TWENTY-FOUR

SABRINA

Two years later

I almost feel as if I'm somewhere else and not at my own wedding. I mean I must be.

There are chickens on the loose.

A spotted horse is eating my wildflowers.

The mother of the groom is in the kitchen baking a pie for some unknown reason.

The makeup artist is late.

And to top everything off, I do believe there's actually a drone in the air.

Following me right this very minute.

I'm on my way to the chicken coop in my favorite terry cloth robe and some flip-flops to investigate why my new family's prized pets are clucking around the seating area for the two hundred plus guests that are about to see me marry the man of my dreams.

I'm not even going to mention this drone thing to Saint, because he'd probably run into his daddy's shed and shoot the thing down with a rifle. I'm pretty sure I know who it belongs to, and the last thing we need is to be sued by The Examiner. Saint's old reporter friend, Myra Kitch, is a senior sports reporter over there now, and she'd just love that. She still has it out for him. Especially nowadays.

"What the fuck is that?" Saint's brother Michael walks up behind me and catches me off guard.

"I think it's a drone," I say while gawking at it.

"The fuck? There's just no honor in journalism anymore. Look at what they've stooped to. There's never been uninvited press at Oak Hill before."

"Don't say that too loudly. You know Saint wanted to elope instead of get married here at home. I don't feel like hearing an, *I told you so.*"

Michael laughs. "That buzzard just wanted to take the quickest path to putting a baby inside of you. Elopement is way faster than how long it took to plan this shindig. I mean you made him wait a year, before he could even propose. You've got a cruel streak in you, sis. I like it."

Everything with Saint is a negotiation. I needed a year to figure out how to manage dating a celebrity athlete while opening a new business. I left Carson Financial and opened my own start-up, but I've got the best two clients in the world: Saint and Spin.

Because of all the change in my life, I told Saint that I wanted us to date an entire year, before we took things to the next level. He granted me that request, and I have to be honest, it was fun. He spent the entire year trying to convince me in very creative ways how it would be in my best interest to lock him down early.

We also both agreed that we wanted children, but my only stipulation with that was that we needed to be married first. My Sunday faithful parents wouldn't be able to sleep at night if I walked down the aisle in a maternity gown. Plus I kind of just wanted it to be the two of us for a while, before we added more humans to the equation. He agreed to that too. Which brings us to where we are now, two years later.

"And why are you out here anyway my beautiful sister-in-law? You should be inside getting ready to marry the bane of my existence. If he knew you were out here worried about all of this, he'd start throwing shit."

"Well right now I'm trying to figure out what to do about *that* thing." I point to the drone. "I made an exclusive deal with *People* magazine for the wedding photos. Three hundred thousand dollars and my reputation are on the line."

"What! Say no more, I'll take care of it, little sis. You just go inside and get pretty."

"I don't know, Mike," I say a little wary of his brand of help. He and Saint were definitely cut from the same cloth. "You can't shoot the thing out of the air. It's actually destruction of private property. I read about a case where a guy actually had to pay the company who was flying a drone over his property."

"Who said I was going to shoot the thing? You've been hanging around Saint too much. Stop worrying. Go inside. I've got this."

"All right." I give him a quick peck on the cheek. "Thanks. Oh and Mike?"

"Yep?"

"The chickens?"

One of the little suckers just went running by.

"That would be a wedding prank courtesy of one Mr. Jake Stevenson. It's his ass backward way of trying to participate. I'll take care of that too."

"Thanks. I'm really going now."
"Good. Go get married. He's waiting."

My New York make up artist never shows up. The jerk. He was supposed to do my makeup and hair, but lucky for me there are two girls on deck to help me with whatever I need on the most important day of my life: Marisol and Kate.

Marisol convinces me to ditch the traditional updo but to wear my hair down in a simple, long-haired bob. The way I always wear it unless it's in a ponytail. It looks elegant and perfect.

Kate is more than excited to do my makeup. While she's on the more adventurous side with her makeup, I'm not, so she decides that I'd look good with an almost bare-faced look except for a soft smoky eye on my lids. When she's finished, I almost want to cry. I love it.

The girls help me slip on my dress. It's a custom made gown by an old seamstress named Mrs. Cavalucci in Brooklyn. It's hand beaded, made from imported Italian silk, and it's the last dress she's ever going to make before retiring.

After securing the final button, the girls leave me

alone for a minute to myself, before the magazine comes in to take a few "pre-wedding" shots of me. A knock about ten minutes later at the door lets me know that they're here.

"One minute," I say.

"Special delivery," A man's voice says.

I crack the door open and see that it's Saint's teammate Cooper instead. I know it's him, because the championship ring on his finger practically blinds me. He hasn't taken it off since receiving it.

"I've got a package for you from your hubby."

Cooper and Saint have become close friends since winning the Superbowl this past winter. It's nice to see that Saint is investing in relationships other than ours, and has someone else to torment on a regular basis.

"You look beautiful by the way."

"Thanks, Coop. What are you eating?" I notice a little piece of something in the corner of his mouth.

"Your mother-in-law is serving mini apple pies as pre-wedding nosh to the guests. Something about it being Robin Robert's new favorite."

"Why?"

"The gunshots frightened a few folks. Mrs. Stevenson said pie would calm everybody down."

"Gunshots?!"

"You didn't hear them? Mike said he had to shoot some dangerous bird that was getting the chickens all riled up."

"The chickens?"

"They're all calm now. Back in the white house where they belong."

Sigh

"All right, Coop, I'll see you down there in a few."

All I can do is laugh while I open up my box.

I guess I know how Mike ended up taking care of the drone. The whole damn family is crazy, but I'm in love with the craziest one of all, and I cannot wait to become his wife. We're going to have an amazing life together.

The box is white and tied with a white ribbon, and there are several things inside.

A lemon.

Two shot glasses.

Some salt.

A bottle of tequila.

A pack of my birth control pills. Crushed and mutilated.

And a small note.

GET READY MRS. GUNSLINGER GAME ON!

♡♡♡

Saint was a fun & flirty ball player, but **WOLF** is a sexy & intense loner full of secrets.

When his quirky personal assistant, Ursula, hands in her resignation, will he realize that he already had the perfect teammate beside him the entire time?

"This is a one-click, *damn I read it one night*, love story!" -ARC reviewer

Grab this super sexy boss romance now.

BOOK LIST

The Masterson Series

Devour this addictive series about the possessive bad boy, Roman Masterson, who falls hard and fast for the girl he's promised his family to protect.

Masterson

Masterson Unleashed

Masterson In Love

Masterson Made

Joseph Loves Juliette

The King Brothers Series

Dive into this series of interconnected standalones featuring 3 alpha hot brothers and the women they lay claim to without apology.

Claimed - Camden & Jade

Indebted - Cutter & Sloan

Broken - Stone & Tiny

Promised - All King Brothers

The Nighthawk Series

Sexy & sweet sports romances set in the professional world of football. All standalones.

Saint - Saint & Sabrina

Wolf - Cooper & Ursula

Diesel - Mason & Olivia

Jett - Jett & Adrienne

Rush - Rush & Mia

The Valencia Mafia Series

Coming Soon. Get Notified!

WHERE YOU CAN FIND ME

MY VIP LIST (Get the nitty gritty)
I have a VIP Reader mailing list. I only send free books, new release, sales or special giveaway info to this group. No spam. Please join here:
http://LisaLangBlakeney.com/VIP

MY PRIVATE FAN GROUP (Casual fun)
Join my private Fan Group on Facebook also known as my "Romance Ninja Warriors" where I share all things new going on, celebrate birthdays, post teasers, yummy pics, giveaways and just chit chat.
http://LisaLangBlakeney.com/community

ACKNOWLEDGMENTS

This is my fourth book, and I am slowly building a team of people who support me tirelessly. So it's time to say thanks...

Thank you to my husband Deric and my daughters for understanding that "free for all" means you have to fix your own dinner, because I'm writing:)

Thank you to my daily group of cheerleaders and champions: Noemi, Tracy, Vicki, Erica, Robin, Kelly, Donna & Stacey. Shout out to my new readers champions: Kim & Anieca

Thank you to my wonderful editor & fellow NYU alumnus: Marla Esposito. Who meets deadlines even when her whole house is sick with a stomach flu.

Special thanks to Deb A Carroll, Johnnie-Marie

Howard, Crystal Gizzard Burnette, Liv Morris and all my other alpha romance ninjas and street ninjas who support me on a daily basis with laughs, encouragement, and spreading the word.

And most of all thank YOU...the reader.

xoxo,

Lisa

ABOUT THE AUTHOR

Lisa Lang
BLAKENEY
Always Alpha Romance

Lisa Lang Blakeney is an international bestselling author of contemporary romance sold in more than 28 countries. Worried that her fellow PTO moms might disapprove, she wrote and published her steamy debut novel Masterson under a different title and pen name in August of 2015.

Thanks to strong reader support of her alpha male character, Roman Masterson, she was encouraged to continue with the series and published the entire Masterson Trilogy the following year. She hasn't looked back since and continues to write novels featuring strong alpha men and the smart women they seek to claim.

A romance junkie for sure, you can find Lisa watching a romantic comedy, reading a romance novel, or writing one of her own most days of the week. If she's not doing that, she's outside in the garden tending to her roses.

Lisa is the wife of one alpha (whom she met in college), mother to four girls, and two labradoodles. Get news on releases, sales and giveaways when you become one of Lisa's VIP readers at : http://LisaLangBlakeney.com/VIP

- facebook.com/authorlisalangblakeney
- twitter.com/LisaLangWrites
- instagram.com/LisaLangBlakeney
- amazon.com/author/lisalangblakeney
- bookbub.com/authors/lisa-lang-blakeney
- goodreads.com/Lisa_Lang_Blakeney
- pinterest.com/lisalangwrites

Printed in Great Britain
by Amazon